Nat Gould

A Gentleman Rider

A tale of the Grand National

Nat Gould

A Gentleman Rider
A tale of the Grand National

ISBN/EAN: 9783337393885

Printed in Europe, USA, Canada, Australia, Japan

Cover: Foto ©Andreas Hilbeck / pixelio.de

More available books at **www.hansebooks.com**

A GENTLEMAN RIDER

A TALE OF THE GRAND NATIONAL

BY

NAT GOULD

AUTHOR OF 'THE DOUBLE EVENT,' ETC.

LONDON

GEORGE ROUTLEDGE AND SONS, LIMITED

BROADWAY, LUDGATE HILL

CONTENTS.

A GENTLEMAN RIDER.

CHAPTER I.

'NOT WHAT IT USED TO BE.'

' FARMING is not what it used to be when I was a lad,' said Charles Massie, 'and I think you would have done better to have gone out to Australia with your uncle William. There's more scope for a young man there, where he is not hampered by so many drawbacks, and has the weather on his side more often than otherwise.'

'Uncle William does not appear to have done much better than you, father,' said his son, Dudley Massie, with a merry twinkle in his eyes.

'Perhaps not,' replied Charles Massie. 'I doubt if he has fared so well; but then William always had bad luck. He's made a living out there; that's more than he would have done here.'

'I am sure Dudley is far better off at home,' said Mary Massie, his sister. 'He is your only son, father, and it would never do for him to leave you.'

'Maybe you're right. I'm a bit of a grumbler, as Sir Gordon says, but he cannot convince me that farming is as good now as it was years ago.'

'You are not a grumbler, and Sir Gordon Sefton has no right to say so,' replied Mary, bridling up at once in defence of her father.

'Don't be hard on Sir Gordon,' said her father; 'he's a good landlord, and he does not mean what he says when he calls me a grumbler. It's a way he has of putting things.'

The Massies, of Five Oaks Farm, were a very old family in Nottinghamshire. Massies had occupied Five Oaks Farm for several centuries, and they bore a more ancient name than that of their landlords, the Seftons. When Sir Gordon Sefton's father purchased Five Oaks Farm from Charlie Massie's father it was a sore blow to the latter to have to sell.

Sir Gordon Sefton's father made his vast wealth in the brewing trade, the Sefton ales being almost as popular as those of Bass. Charlie Massie's father paid more attention to racing and various other sports than to farming, and consequently he lost money faster than Sir Gordon's father made it.

When Sir Gordon's father bid for Five Oaks Farm, Massie, much as he stood in need of the money, declined to sell without an agreement to the effect that he was to remain on the farm, and his son Charles was to have it after him.

Having purchased a large estate adjoining Five Oaks Farm, Mr. Sefton (Sir Gordon was the first baronet) was anxious to improve the property by including Massie's farm in it. Rich men generally manage to have their own way in such matters when they have to deal with men short of money. Mr. Sefton agreed to Massie's terms, and the farm was sold.

When Charles Massie became tenant of Five Oaks Farm on the death of his father, Sir Gordon Sefton, whose father was also dead, had been made a baronet about three or four years. Had Sir Gordon's father lived, he would undoubtedly have received the honour, for he had given princely gifts to various charities, and was generally regarded as a philanthropist. Having piled up his enormous wealth mainly out of the pockets of the working and middle classes, he decided to return to them, in this form, a small portion of their contributions.

Sir Gordon's father was what might be called a self-made man, who had not received a too brilliant education. Knowing lack of education was a serious drawback in social life, he took care his son Gordon should have the best education it was possible to give him.

Sir Gordon went to Eton, and from there to Oxford, and, although he did not turn out a brilliant scholar, he had the polish of the university upon him. Although not of an old family, Sir Gordon Sefton was a gentleman, with gentlemanly tastes and pursuits. He married well, his wife coming of an aristocratic stock, and bringing with her a considerable dowry. It was a love match, and Lady Sefton's parents, at first opposed to the union, had to give way. It was a happy marriage, and Lady Sefton at forty-five was as much attached to her husband as when she married him at the early age of twenty

Charles Massie, soon after he became tenant of Five Oaks Farm, received a legacy of several thousands of pounds from a distant relative in America, who, probably believing him to be the only son of his father, had left William Massie out in the cold.

'Just your uncle Will's luck,' as Charles Massie said when alluding to the matter to his children.

On receiving this money, Charles Massie wished to repurchase Five Oaks Farm. He was good friends with Sir Gordon Sefton, who recognised in him a man of old family and sterling worth. Sir Gordon would have gone out of his way to oblige Charles Massie, but he could not bring himself to resell the farm.

Charles Massie argued with Sir Gordon, but all to no purpose. On this one point he was obstinate.

'What am I to do with the money,' said Charles Massie, 'if you decline to sell the farm ?'

Sir Gordon laughed as he said :

'I fancy you can easily find a better invest-ment for it than putting it into Five Oaks Farm.'

'But it's the farm I want,' said Charles Massie.

'And it's the farm I cannot let you have,' replied Sir Gordon. 'Come, Mr. Massie, give up the idea. I am not a bad landlord, and you are an excellent tenant, and we get on very well together. Let things remain as they are, and say no more about it.'

'The Massies have been here some hundreds of years, Sir Gordon,' said Mr. Massie. 'My father unfortunately had to sell. Be generous, and let me buy back what your father bought from us.'

It was rather a sore point with Lady Gordon and her daughter Ena, this 'old family' of the Massies. As for Sir Gordon, his son, and younger daughter, Beatrice, they cared very little about it.

'I am sorry to refuse your request,' said Sir Gordon; 'but it need not cause any strained feelings between us. You are almost as much master of the farm as though it were your own.'

Seeing Sir Gordon would not give way, Charles Massie dropped the subject.

'We are going to float the Sefton breweries into a company,' said Sir Gordon; 'and if you care to put your money into the concern, I will see it is done. It will be a fine investment for you, and yield you a handsome percentage.'

Charles Massie had taken Sir Gordon's advice, and for many years had drawn a dividend of from ten to nearly twenty per cent. on his money.

This irregular income made Charles Massie

more independent than most farmers in the neighbourhood, and enabled him to give his son and daughter an excellent education.

Five Oaks Farm was a fine property, and although Charles Massie said farming was not what it used to be, he had no cause to complain. The farm was situated within easy distance of that famous district in Nottinghamshire known as Sherwood Forest and the Dukeries. The house was picturesque and old-fashioned, roomy, and of somewhat stately appearance for a farm-house. It resembled an old manor house whose owner had deserted it for a more modern abode.

Dudley Massie had already made a name for himself as a gentleman rider, and his father was rather proud of it than otherwise. Although fond of hunting and racing, he did not neglect home pursuits, and was a great help to his father.

It was through the influence of Sir Gordon Sefton that Dudley Massie had been elected a member of Sir Gordon's club, which gave him the necessary qualification to join the ranks of gentleman riders. Young Massie, Sir Gordon knew, was a thorough gentleman, and as regards his family, it was considerably more ancient than his own. Consequently he had no hesitation in proposing him as a member of the rather exclusive club to which he belonged. Sir Gordon was a popular man at his club, and Dudley Massie was elected without any trouble. At this club Dudley Massie made many new acquaintances, and his fame as a horseman having become known, he received many good mounts. The year before our story commences Dudley Massie's name stood third on the list of successful gentlemen riders, and his reputation was high as a thoroughly capable and reliable horseman.

Dudley Massie took good care his name should not be mixed up in any of the shady transactions that mar the fair fame of some so-called gentlemen riders. He declined many good mounts because he did not care for the men owning the horses, and consequently, in certain quarters, he was called a prig, and not regarded with any favour. It is well-nigh impossible for such a man as Dudley Massie not to make enemies of certain men on the turf—and that he had enemies he knew full well. He carefully concealed this from his father because he did not wish to cause him any uneasiness. He had ridden against men whose reputations were good, but he knew them for what they were worth, and had on more than one occasion perhaps rashly expressed his

opinion of their riding. It was not from any
desire on his part to be meddlesome, but
Dudley Massie's feelings revolted at anything
he considered unfair. He saw things done in
races that fairly made his blood boil, and he
despised the men who, under the cover of the
'gentleman rider,' resorted to tricks no professional jockey dared attempt. Dudley Massie
rode for the honour of winning, and reaped no
reward from the owner of the horse, although
he often had a 'pony' or so on his mount. A
more fearless rider never got into a saddle.
Even his enemies acknowledged this. Many a
race had he won by good judgment, and he felt
pleased when one of the best jockeys of his day
said to him after a race : 'I couldn't have ridden
a better finish myself, Mr. Massie. It was a
splendid race !'

Dudley Massie could not afford to keep more
than one horse at Five Oaks Farm for purely
racing purposes under National Hunt rules.

Sir Gordon Sefton, however, had several
good horses, and Dudley Massie had the choice
of a mount at any meet near at hand during the
hunting season.

Arthur Sefton, much to the grief of his
parents, was a cripple. His spine had been
injured when he was quite a child, and he was

unable to walk.   Arthur Sefton and Dudley
Massie were fast friends.   The crippled lad—
he was eighteen—seemed to delight in hearing
of the feats performed by his friend, the more
so as he was utterly incapacitated from attempt-
ing them himself.   He gloried in the healthy
manhood of Dudley Massie, and although he
often regarded Dudley with longing, wistful
eyes, he never murmured or complained.

It was chiefly on Arthur Sefton's account
that Dudley Massie became such a constant
visitor at the Seftons'

Lady Sefton considered the Massies were
not on the same footing in society as the
Seftons, nor were they, although the Massie
pedigree would have compared more than
favourably with that of the Seftons.   She was
not haughty to Dudley Massie, but he knew
the feeling she had towards him, and smiled
at it.   Lady Sefton would have been highly
indignant had she known that her ' little ways '
amused Dudley Massie instead of annoying
him.

Mary Massie and Beatrice Sefton were also
great friends, but Ena Sefton was too much
like her mother, and was rather condescending
towards her sister's friend.   Arthur Sefton never
regretted his crippled state more than when he

watched the graceful form of Mary Massie as she walked about the grounds with his sister Beatrice.

Something more than mere chance had thrown these families together.

CHAPTER II.

THE SEFTONS' HEIR.

'I wish Dudley would come,' said Arthur Sefton, as he lay on his invalid's carriage on the lawn at Sefton House. 'Do you think he will be long?'

'They are shooting to-day,' replied his sister Beatrice, 'and Mr. Massie has joined them, at father's request, or he would have been here now. Do you miss him very much?'

'Oh yes,' replied Arthur. 'Dudley is such a good fellow. He never grumbles, and never tires of talking to me; besides, he has such good spirits. Do you know, Beaty, he almost makes me forget I am a wretched cripple when he talks to me; some of his healthy manhood seems to come upon me as I listen to him. You like Dudley, do you not?' he asked quickly, looking hard at his sister.

2

Beatrice Sefton blushed, and looked away from her brother as she replied :

' I think Mr Massie is a very nice man, and I like him very much because he is so kind to you.'

' You are very good to me,' said Arthur, caressing her hand.   'You understand me better than Ena, better than mother, better than all of them.   I should be very lonely if you left me.'

' I am not likely to leave you,' she replied. ' What made you say so ?'

' Because beautiful girls have lovers, who develop, in time, into husbands, and then crippled brothers and such-like encumbrances are forgotten,' he replied.

Beatrice Sefton laughed heartily as she said :

' You flatter me, Arthur.   Ena is the beauty of our family, and exacts all the homage of the male sex who visit here.   There is no fear of my leaving you, and I have no wish to do so.'

Arthur Sefton was silent for a few moments, and a spasm of pain shot across his face. Beatrice saw it, and at once placed her arms under his shoulders, and raised him into a more comfortable position.   A sigh of satisfaction from Arthur rewarded her.

' I have discovered a secret,' he said.

' Does it concern me ?' asked Beatrice.

' No ; I wish it did,' he replied. ' I do not think others have noticed it. Ena may have done ; but she is so mighty proud, it would only annoy her. I am afraid I shall end by cordially disliking Ena, and that would not be a proper state of feeling for a brother to have towards his sister.'

' Ena is proud,' said Beatrice ; ' but she is very fond of you, although, perhaps, she does not show it in the same way that I do. Ena has to help mother in her social duties, while I, as the younger sister, have more time to devote to you.'

Again Arthur Sefton remained silent, and then said quietly :

' I think, Beaty, I may tell you ; but you will not mention it, because I may be wrong. I want your opinion. Two heads are better than one, and your head is a particularly clear one, my sister. You know how much I value Dudley's friendship, and how good he always is to me. I am afraid he is on the wrong track, a track that may cause him pain, and wound his pride ; for he has a proper pride in himself, although he is not haughty or overbearing. It would hurt him very much to be slighted.'

2—2

'What do you mean?' asked his sister. 'No one at Sefton would think of slighting Mr. Massie.'

'Beatrice,' he said earnestly, 'I think Dudley admires Ena; now, if it were yourself—— What have I said, Beaty?' he exclaimed, noticing the startled, timid look in his sister's face.

'You surprised me,' she replied. 'Mr. Massie admire Ena! I never noticed it myself. I think you are mistaken.'

I hope I am,' replied Arthur. 'But now you see what I mean when I say Dudley might be hurt and slighted.'

Beatrice Sefton was silent. A sudden change had come over her; she could hardly define it. She had been thrown much more into Dudley Massie's society than her sister Ena, and she had come to regard him with kindly feelings because he was so attentive to Arthur. This sudden discovery, that possibly Dudley Massie might admire Ena, caused her pain. Why it caused her pain she hardly knew as yet. She knew Ena would not regard Dudley Massie with favour as an admirer, but would consider it presumption on his part to entertain such feelings towards her.

Arthur Sefton watched her attentively, but did not divine what was passing in her mind.

'What do you think Ena would say if she knew ?' he asked.

'Ena is so different from many girls,' replied Beatrice. 'Most girls would be proud of the friendship of such a man as your friend Mr. Massie. Mother expects Ena to make a brilliant marriage, and she has been educated up to that standard.'

'Thank goodness you have not !' said Arthur. 'Mother has made a grave mistake with Ena. It's lucky for you she has not tried any experiments upon you in that direction. I think I'll give Dudley a hint.'

'I should not do that,' said Beatrice quickly. 'It is not wise to interfere in such matters, and, after all, you may be mistaken.'

'You are right,' he said ; 'I will not mention it ; but now I have told you, I think you will have no difficulty in noticing it. Wheel me down the drive, there's a good girl. They are sure to return that way.'

Beatrice wheeled the carriage slowly along the drive until they came to the lodge-gates. A magnificent view was to be had from Sefton House lodge. Rich pasture-land stretched far away in front, until it almost touched the boundaries of the famous forest of Sherwood. Five Oaks Farm lay to the right, surrounded by the five ancient giant oaks from which it derived its name. Sefton House was not exactly one of the show-places of the Dukeries, like Welbeck, Thoresby, or Rufford Abbey, but it was a splendid mansion, and no man dispensed hospitality with a more liberal hand than Sir Gordon Sefton. Arthur Sefton loved to feast his eyes on this beautiful landscape. He never wearied of it, and always found some new feature of interest in it.

Robert Finchley, the lodge-keeper, often chatted with the heir of the Seftons as he lay in his carriage at the gates.

Bob Finchley was head-gamekeeper to Sir Gordon until he lost his right arm in an affray with a desperate gang of Nottingham poachers.

Being a married man, Sir Gordon appointed him to the lodge after the accident, and he had occupied the position for some years.

When Bob Finchley saw the carriage approaching, he went out and stood by the gate. He never missed speaking to Arthur Sefton if he could help it.

'When will the shooting-party return?' asked Arthur.

'I heard the guns about half an hour back,' said Bob; 'they were shooting at Five Oaks then. I do not expect they will be long : they generally wind up at the farm.'

' Plenty of birds this year ?' asked Arthur.

' A splendid lot ; it makes me wish I was among 'em again,' said Bob Finchley, with a sigh.

' I'm sorry for you, Bob,' said Arthur ; ' but you are better off than I am. Oh, what would I not give to be able to walk about !'

There was almost a tone of anguish in his voice, that touched both Beatrice and Bob Finchley.

' I ought not to grumble, Mr. Arthur,' he said ; ' I ought to have more patience. You set us all a good example.'

' That he does,' said Beatrice ; ' and some day, perhaps, he will have his reward. Dr. Hart thinks you may get stronger as you grow older.'

' Then Dr. Hart is wrong,' said Arthur. ' You need not try to bolster me up with false hopes. I am on my back, and likely to remain there. Ah ! here they come.'

Four gentlemen came up the road, followed by a couple of keepers and several dogs. They were Sir Gordon Sefton, Dudley Massie, Morgan Sherburn, and Fred Lostock. They grouped themselves round Arthur's carriage, and began to relate what sort of sport they had experienced.

Sir Gordon Sefton dearly loved his crippled son and heir, and, although his heart was heavy as he thought how the lad was cut off from so many manly enjoyments, he never showed the pain he felt in his face.

Arthur Sefton did not like Morgan Sherburn, nor did Beatrice. Morgan Sherburn was a very wealthy young man, of a good North-Country family, and chief partner in one of the great iron foundries of the Newcastle district. His income was enormous, and he had the reputation of spending it in the most extravagant manner.

Dudley Massie was surprised to find Morgan Sherburn on such intimate terms with the Seftons, and Morgan Sherburn wondered why Sir Gordon tolerated 'such a fellow as Massie.'

Morgan Sherburn was devoted to racing, and was near the top of the tree as a gentleman rider. He had a most extensive establishment at Newmarket, a fine house in Park Lane, two or three country seats, kept a most luxuriously-fitted yacht, and was a member of some expensive clubs.

Dudley Massie, however, knew his reputation was not good, and that his character would not bear strict investigation. To all outward appearances, Morgan Sherburn was a gentleman at present, but it was doubtful whether his associations would not wear off the gloss in time.

Fred Lostock was a son of Admiral Lostock, but, unlike his father, had taken to business instead of the sea.

When the usual greetings were over, Sir Gordon and Dudley Massie walked with Arthur and Beatrice, the other two going on in front.

'Let me wheel the carriage,' said Dudley.

'Do, there's a good fellow,' said Arthur; 'I am sure Beaty must be tired. She is awfully good to me.'

'I am sure she is,' said Dudley. 'We all try our best to please you. I wish we could do more for you.'

'I have one advantage over a strong man like you,' said Arthur; 'I always find other people to do all my work for me. How many brace did you bag to-day, and who shot the most birds?'

'We bagged twenty brace and an odd one,' said Sir Gordon, 'and, as usual, Mr. Massie headed the list.'

'How many did you kill?'

'Eight brace,' said Dudley; 'but I missed several easy shots.'

'Massie shoots well,' said Fred Lostock to Morgan Sherburn.

'He's not a bad shot, and he's a fairly good rider. As far as I know, those are his only qualifications to be admitted into Sefton's society,' replied Sherburn.

Fred Lostock thought to himself, 'I don't think your qualifications are any better,' and added aloud :

'He nearly beat you in the list of winning riders last season ; you were only three above him. Have you anything good for the coming fray ?'

'I have several good ones, and mean to have a cut in for the Grand National. Massie had a lot of luck in his mounts last season. I do not think he will get so many wins again. Ah! there's Miss Sefton. Fine girl, is she not ? A regular thoroughbred to look at, and quite as haughty. I should not care to offend her. I fancy she would hold her own with any man.'

'She is a handsome woman,' said Lostock, 'but I prefer her sister.'

'Don't admire your taste, then,' replied Morgan Sherburn.

Ena Sefton justified the expression that she was a handsome woman. She was tall and stately, and had her mother's good looks and aristocratic features. Her movements were graceful, and she could, when she so pleased, be affable and gracious. Ena Sefton had a very good opinion of herself and her charms, and knew she was generally admired. She did not care much for Morgan Sherburn ; but then he was a millionaire, and that made all the difference. Ena Sefton had a full appreciation of the value of money. She greeted the gentlemen without any particular show of cordiality.

Beatrice Sefton, as she saw her sister on the lawn, thought of what her brother had said, and looked at Dudley Massie. She saw he was looking at Ena with ill-disguised admiration, and somehow she felt dissatisfied that he did so. A glance at Ena, however, showed Beatrice that her sister did not notice Dudley Massie's looks, and this gave her a sense of relief.

As Dudley Massie shook hands with Ena Sefton, Arthur whispered to his sister :

' Dudley never appears to see anyone when Ena is present ; it makes quite a different man of him. Why cannot Ena leave him alone ?

She ought not to want all the men in the place to fall down and worship her!'

These remarks were unjust to Ena Sefton, who never gave more than a passing thought to Dudley Massie.

CHAPTER III.

MORGAN SHERBURN.

WHEN Morgan Sherburn's father died, the young man inherited vast wealth, and a very large amount of it was in ready money. Sherburn's iron foundry had a world-wide reputation, and the income Morgan Sherburn derived from this source alone was a fortune in itself every year.

During his father's lifetime, Morgan Sherburn's income had not been large. His father was a shrewd business man, and would not tolerate extravagance in his family.

Morgan Sherburn found it necessary at this period to race under an assumed name ; but no sooner was his father dead than he threw off the thin disguise, and entered and rode horses in his own name. He had always been a man of expensive tastes and habits, and to gratify these before his father's death he borrowed money at the usual high rate of interest. The vast fortune he inherited, however, made it an easy matter to settle old scores without any perceptible drain upon his resources. The money-lenders were paid in full, and wished they had dealt more liberally with him.

Morgan Sherburn gradually developed into a rather vicious man. His mode of life did not bear close inspection. He cared very little for the feelings of others, so long as he could have his own way. Money in the hands of such a man is a curse not only to himself, but to others. The fortune his father had amassed he would have squandered in a very short time had his wealth not been so enormous. Although he had very little capacity for business, he was a shrewd man in his turf dealings, and not over-scrupulous. He kept horses for his own benefit and pleasure, and considered the public were fools, and ought therefore to part freely with their money.

Morgan Sherburn, when in London, was fond of mixing with men and women much below his station in life, although their manners were often even better than his own. He frequented the company of fighting-men, and was well known to many of the leaders of that doubtful class of women who reap a rich, if fleeting, harvest in the great city. He was a vain man in many respects, but it was a low class of vanity that possessed him. He loved to hear his name coupled with that of some reigning stage beauty, and he could generally outbid all competitors for her favour. Upon the favourite of the hour he lavished money in the most extravagant fashion. He bought and paid heavily for these doubtful privileges.

Mixing with men and women of this class does not tend to improve either mind or manners. Morgan Sherburn's mind had long been vitiated, but he still retained some of the outward manner of a gentleman. He was careful, however, to conceal his town life from such an acquaintance as Sir Gordon Sefton, who regarded Morgan Sherburn favourably for his father's sake.

Dudley Massie, however, knew more of Morgan Sherburn than that individual thought. A racing man such as Sherburn was could not keep secret many of his transactions, and Dudley Massie had heard of some shady things that had been done in Sherburn's name, and presumably with his sanction.

Fred Lostock was a very different man from Morgan Sherburn, whom he rather despised.

' Don't you think you are making very bad use of your money ?' he had ventured to say to Morgan Sherburn when he heard of some more extravagant piece of folly than usual.

' I am gratifying my own desires ; if you call that making a bad use of my money, I differ from you,' was the reply.

' I often gratify my own desires,' replied Fred Lostock, ' but I never put such a high price upon them.'

' That is because you cannot afford to,' said Sherburn. ' Men are all alike. It is merely a question of money as to whether one man goes the pace faster than another.'

Fred Lostock did not continue the argument. He was not a hypocrite, and he believed there was a certain amount of truth in Sherburn's contention.

Morgan Sherburn, until he met Ena Sefton, had an idea that all women were alike in one respect—dazzled by his great wealth. Ena Sefton was too wise to show him what she thought of his millions. She was anything but dazzled by them ; on the contrary, she rather overshadowed Sherburn's millions when in his presence. The rich young man had been so accustomed to conquest that he was piqued at Ena Sefton's evident control over herself.

Fond mothers on the look-out for eligible suitors to their daughters had flung the young damsels, so to speak, at the rich man's feet, and some of them had been trampled on and a little damaged in the process. Not that they allowed Morgan Sherburn to have entirely his own way, but they compromised themselves with him in the hope of hooking the valuable fish with the tempting bait. These expert anglers in the matrimonial stream had discovered that although the fish rose to the fly with alacrity, he declined to be hooked, although he tried hard to take the bait and evade the consequences. It requires great patience and a large amount of finesse to become a successful angler, and Ena Sefton possessed both attributes. Not that she angled for Morgan Sherburn. She considered herself far superior to him, but she knew his millions were solid, and this weighed with her.

Lady Sefton did not like Morgan Sherburn, because she saw that under the outward garb of the gentleman were concealed feelings she detested and abhorred. She was rather surprised when Ena replied, in answer to her question as to what she thought of Morgan Sherburn

' He is a millionaire, mother, and therefore

cannot be judged as an ordinary man. Personally, I am rather amused at him. As a man he is not a very desirable *parti;* as a millionaire he would be a very useful appendage.'

' He admires you very much, I am sure,' said Lady Sefton.

' Possibly on account of my being different from the general run of his acquaintances of my sex,' said Ena.

' Really, Ena, you don't suppose——' commenced her mother.

' My dear mother, Mr. Sherburn is a man and a millionaire, and therefore he must have a very wide choice,' said Ena.

From this conversation it will be seen that Ena Sefton was fully alive to the class of man Morgan Sherburn was. It cannot therefore be argued that in her subsequent conduct she acted with her eyes closed to his faults.

The more Morgan Sherburn saw of Ena Sefton, the more he admired her. She did not encourage him in the least, and this made him more anxious to secure her favour. He had not as yet begun to think of marriage in connection with Ena Sefton or any other woman. He was not a marrying man, but to possess such a woman as Ena he would have gone to any length, even to surrendering his bachelor liberty. The time for this had not arrived yet, but he was becoming more infatuated with this handsome, haughty, well-bred woman every time he saw her. Miss Marie de Tourville of the Gaiety was all very well in her way, but she paled into insignificance when placed beside Ena Sefton.

Morgan Sherburn remained a couple of days at Sefton House, and when he left he knew, or thought he knew, that neither his millions nor himself had made much impression upon Miss Sefton.

It was a relief to him when he reached London to listen to the false flatteries and wheedling endearments of Marie de Tourville, whose real name, hidden beneath this flowery covering, was Flossie Griggs. He had to pay heavily for Marie de Tourville's society, but he did not mind the expense so long as his sense of vanity and conquest was satisfied. Whatever Miss de Tourville's abilities on the stage might be—and they appeared limited to high kicking and wearing elegant costumes—she was an adept in the art of extracting money from well-filled pockets in a legitimate and perfectly legal manner.

The evening Morgan Sherburn returned to

town from Sefton House the fair Miss de Tourville was the recipient of a handsome diamond ring from him. After a 'little supper' she politely asked him for a loan to carry her over the week, and when this was secured, said a new brougham and a pair of showy horses would look well waiting for her when the theatre was over.

Morgan Sherburn was rather amused than otherwise at the demands she made upon him, but he paid her out by saying :

'Do you know, my fair Marie, you are becoming quite *passée.* I have been in the country, and the beauties there are enchanting. You really ought to have a week or two in the country. Just imagine what it would save you in rouge and other articles of embellishment !'

'Go on,' she said ; 'you don't mean it ! You are chaffing, Morgan. Look me in the face and say I'm not charming, if you dare.'

The challenge proved fatal, and Morgan Sherburn blandly acknowledged defeat.

In his own house, however, Morgan Sherburn felt disgusted with such women as Marie de Tourville when he thought of Ena Sefton.

He knew Miss Sefton would be hard to rule, and that she would want to hold the reins in

case she married him.   He was good at making
promises which were easily broken.

'If I do marry you, my haughty lady,' he
said to himself—'that is, if I ask you and you
will have me—we can arrange matters after the
ceremony.   I don't flatter myself you would
fall ardently in love with me, and although I
admire you very much, you are too much of an
iceberg to be melted in a few days or even
weeks.   But you are a very handsome woman,
and would do me credit.   If we quarrelled at
home, I think I could tame you.   I have had
some refractory horses to deal with in my time,
and generally came off victor, and I think I
could manage you.   Hang me if I shouldn't
feel quite proud to hear such remarks, as you
drove in the Park, as, " By Jove! what a
splendid woman!   Who is she?"   " Morgan
Sherburn's wife.   She's much too good for
him, although he is a millionaire." '

He chuckled at the bare thought of the
dismay of certain ladies of his acquaintance
when they first saw the haughty Ena Sefton as
his wife.

He wanted Ena Sefton merely to gratify his
vanity and to reflect a certain glory upon
himself.

'She's much too proud to do anything to

lower herself,' he said. 'She could go her way, and I would go mine. She would not mind such an arrangement, I feel sure. As to money —well, there's any amount of it, and she might have her share. She might object to some of my escapades, but she'd get used to them in time.'

Morgan Sherburn had hardly gauged Ena Sefton's character correctly. Probably she would not have objected to some such arrangement as Morgan Sherburn contemplated in regard to their individual freedom, but she would have indignantly denounced any open infidelity that would have touched her good name through him.

Had Ena Sefton taken the trouble to reckon up the merits of Dudley Massie and Morgan Sherburn, her innate sense of honesty would have made her unhesitatingly declare in favour of the former. This would not, however, have overshadowed the fact that Sherburn had millions and Massie had but a few thousands. Sir Gordon Sefton would have declared unreservedly in favour of Dudley Massie, had he been called upon to choose between them. Lady Sefton might have hesitated, but eventually she would have sided, like Ena, with Sherburn's millions.

CHAPTER IV

A NEW PURCHASE.

' MR. SHERBURN once owned this horse, and I think he made a mistake in parting with him,' said Fred Bexley, the well-known horse-dealer, to Dudley Massie as they stood together contemplating a fine upstanding dark bay horse in one of the dealer's horse-boxes at Nottingham.

Dudley Massie was on the look-out for a horse for Sir Gordon Sefton, an animal likely to have a chance in good company, over the sticks, and one that might possibly win a Grand National. Such horses are not picked up without a good deal of looking for, and Dudley Massie had been all over the Midlands searching for the kind of horse he required. He had dealt with Bexley on many occasions, and found him a straightforward man.

Fred Bexley was a curious mixture of shrewdness and honesty. He dearly loved making a good bargain, and perhaps in some cases his honesty would have been considered plastic. He never wittingly told a falsehood about a horse when asked a question, but he was not above concealing a horse's faults if a purchaser did not touch upon them.

Dudley Massie liked the looks of this horse, but he could not imagine what had induced Morgan Sherburn to part with him. He knew Sherburn was a good judge, and seldom sold an animal that afterwards turned out well. When he had a good horse Morgan Sherburn kept it.

' I wonder why Mr. Sherburn sold him,' said Dudley Massie. ' Did you purchase the horse from him ?'

' No,' replied Bexley. ' The horse was bought after winning a selling race, and I believe it was owing to some misunderstanding that Mr. Sherburn lost him. I know he tried to buy him back, but the purchaser and Mr. Sherburn were not on very good terms, and consequently there was no deal. I bought the horse about a month ago. He has been "spelling" nearly all the summer, and is not in first-class condition, as you see, but there is nothing wrong with him, and I have ridden him several times.'

' Have you had him over the hurdles ?' asked Dudley.

' Yes, and he fences well ; but, of course, he is a bit out of practice,' replied Bexley.

' I think he is the sort of horse to suit Sir Gordon,' said Dudley ; ' but you are asking a stiff price for him.'

'He's worth it, and more,' said Bexley. 'I assure you I shall have no difficulty in selling him for three hundred guineas. He's six years old, and sound as a bell.'

'How is he bred?' asked Dudley.

'By Bendigo out of Dewdrop. He is un-named, I believe. Ran as the Dewdrop colt. It is rather a weakness of Mr. Sherburn's, not naming his horses,' said Fred Bexley.

'By Jove! I remember him now,' said Dudley. 'He won a good race at Derby, and Sherburn rode him. It was a hunters' flat race, I think, and the horse beat a big field.'

'So you know him, eh?' said Bexley, smiling. 'I ought to have put a stiffer price on him, I'm a generous man, Mr. Massie. Some people call horse-dealers hard names; they ought to couple mine with something a bit soft.'

'A man would have to be up extra early in the morning to get the better of you,' said Dudley 'If you warrant the horse in the usual way, I'll buy him.'

'It's a deal, then,' said Fred Bexley; 'and I wish Sir Gordon luck with him. I suppose you will train him yourself?'

'Yes,' replied Dudley. 'Sir Gordon prefers his horses trained privately — I mean his jumpers. He has several flat racers in training at Newmarket, but I do not think he takes very much interest in them.'

'Shall I deliver the horse at Sefton House? said Bexley. 'I can send him over to-morrow.'

'That will do,' replied Dudley Massie; 'and Sir Gordon will forward you a cheque.'

'Oh, the cash will do any time,' said Bexley. 'I wish Sir Gordon owed me a few thousands.'

When the new purchase arrived at Sefton House, Sir Gordon was well pleased with the horse, and considered him cheap at the price.

'Curious that Morgan Sherburn should have owned him,' he said. 'Perhaps he will want to buy him back from me. I shall not feel inclined to sell if the horse proves as good as he looks.'

Dudley Massie was not long in putting the horse through his paces, and trying him over the hurdles.

Sir Gordon had made a fine training track at Sefton, and the fences were of a sufficient stiffness to make a horse jump at his best.

It was on Dudley Massie's advice these fences had been put up. He knew it made a horse slovenly and careless in his work if the jumps were too easy. If Sir Gordon's horses lacked pace occasionally, they always jumped well, and owing to this won many races over more speedy horses.

Being by Bendigo out of such a speedy mare as Dewdrop, it was no matter for surprise that the new purchase possessed pace.   The way he moved over the ground gave Dudley Massie great satisfaction, and he knew that in the son of Bendigo he had purchased something out of the common for Sir Gordon.

Arthur Sefton was often wheeled down to the track, in his carriage, in order to see the horses at work.   When he saw the new purchase he gave expression to his delight in the most unmistakable manner.   As Dudley Massie went past on the horse Arthur waved his hand for him to go faster, and, nothing loath, Dudley let the horse extend himself, and he dashed round the track at a great pace.   If the horse had a fault, it was in his mouth.   He had a hard mouth, and a habit of pulling when fully extended, that was by no means pleasant for his rider.   He was not, however, a horse that, when he had done pulling, had done racing.

'What a fine goer he is!' said Arthur Sefton as Massie led the horse up to him.   'What is his name?'

'He does not possess one yet,' said Dudley 'Can you suggest anything?   He is by Bendigo out of Dewdrop.   Something in the fighting line would be appropriate.'

'Call him The Slogger,' said Arthur, smiling.

'A jolly good name for him,' said Dudley. 'Mention it to Sir Gordon. I am sure he will be only too pleased you have chosen a name for him.'

Sir Gordon Sefton, seeing how boyishly pleased his son was over the name he had chosen, agreed to it, and the new purchase was called The Slogger.

About a week after Dudley Massie bought The Slogger for Sir Gordon Sefton, Morgan Sherburn came down to Nottingham, and paid a visit to Fred Bexley.

'I hear you have a horse I formerly owned, Bexley. He's by Bendigo out of Dewdrop. I wish to buy him back. What's your price?'

'My price *was* three hundred guineas,' said Fred Bexley

'*Was!*' exclaimed Morgan Sherburn. 'What do you mean ? Have you raised the price, then?'

'No ; I sold him last week for that amount,' said Bexley

Morgan Sherburn made use of language that Fred Bexley thought almost too forcible even for a millionaire. After sundry expletives, he asked to whom the horse had been sold.

'Mr. Massie bought him for Sir Gordon Sefton,' said Fred Bexley, 'and I don't fancy you have much chance of getting him from there.'

Morgan Sherburn was in a very bad humour. He no sooner learned that Fred Bexley had the horse than he came down to buy him, and instead of getting what he desired, he found the horse sold to the man of all others he wished not to have him.   It was not that he cared so much for Sir Gordon Sefton owning the horse, but he knew Dudley Massie would have the mounts on him.

'If it had not been for that blundering fool of a trainer of mine, I should never have lost the horse.   He put someone up to bid for him after a selling race, and the fellow made a mess of it and let him go,' said Morgan Sherburn.

'You seem precious sorry to have lost him,' said Fred Bexley.   'He must be an uncommon good horse.'

'He's a good horse for a man who understands him, and knows his peculiarities,' said Sherburn.   'Massie will never do any good with him.   I must try and induce Sir Gordon to let me have him back.'

'What faults has he got?' said Fred Bexley. 'I did not discover any.   He pulls a trifle, and has a hardish mouth; but there's nothing much the matter with him.'

'You have not ridden him in races, and I have,' said Morgan Sherburn.

'If the horse has to be ridden in a certain way you had better give Sir Gordon Sefton a hint about it,' said Bexley.

'I'm likely to do that,' said Sherburn. 'No, my wily Bexley, that's not my way, and it's not your way; so do not try and make me think you are an innocent cherub, because it will not wash.'

'If all I hear's correct,' said Bexley, 'I am an innocent cherub, as you put it, compared to yourself.'

Morgan Sherburn laughed. He considered Fred Bexley's remarks complimentary rather than otherwise.

'I don't want a journey for nothing, any way,' he said. 'Have you anything in your stables worth buying?'

'I have several horses good enough for most men, but they may not suit you. You are a trifle difficult to deal with, Mr. Sherburn,' said Bexley.

'Know too much for you, eh?' said Sherburn. 'You're about right there. I reckon it would take a smarter man than even you are, Mr. Bexley, to sell me a screw.'

'I never have screws in my stables,' said

Bexley; 'but I'll show you what I have got, and, being such an excellent judge, I have no doubt you will pick the best out.'

They walked round the stables, and Morgan Sherburn saw there were two or three useful-looking horses of the stamp he required. He was wroth at Dudley Massie for purchasing the horse he had come down to buy, and he thought it would be a good joke to buy an animal out of Bexley's stables that would prove the superior. He fancied he knew exactly what the son of Bendigo could do, and one horse in Bexley's stables looked good enough to beat him.

'This gray horse is a fair animal,' he said.

'You've picked the best,' said Fred Bexley. 'He is a good horse, and a well-bred one to boot. He's called Snowstorm, and he's by a son of Hermit out of Storm. His mother was a gray mare. You may remember her. She won at Lincoln and Nottingham in her time.'

'How much for him?' asked Morgan Sherburn.

'Five hundred guineas,' said Bexley.

'Two hundred more than the Bendigo fellow. You always had a cast-iron nerve, Bexley.'

'He's worth it,' said Bexley. 'That's my price.'

'I'll give you four hundred,' said Sherburn.

Fred Bexley knew his man. He would have asked Dudley Massie a much less price for Snowstorm, but he was certain, if Morgan Sherburn wanted to buy the horse, the price would not stop him.

After some haggling a bargain was struck, and Snowstorm became the property of Morgan Sherburn for four hundred and fifty guineas.

'You do not know when you have got hold of a good horse,' said Sherburn.

'You do, evidently,' replied Bexley.

'I think the gray will be able to take down the bay's number if they happen to meet,' said Sherburn.

'Is that what you have bought him for?' asked Fred Bexley.

'If I cannot buy the one I want from Sir Gordon, it will be some satisfaction to know I found one in the same stables to beat him,' said Morgan Sherburn.

When Morgan Sherburn left, Fred Bexley thought over what he had said, and laughed to himself over the prospect of Snowstorm beating the son of Bendigo.

'They say you are very clever at racing, Mr. Sherburn,' he said to himself. 'You may be quite as clever as some folk give you credit for, but I fancy you'll discover the bay will beat the gray, or my name's not Bexley.'

CHAPTER V.

THE SLOGGER HAS PECULIARITIES.

THE SLOGGER had one or two peculiarities that Dudley Massie found it difficult to understand. He could hardly put them down to bad temper, because, taken all round, the horse did not show much temper. At first Dudley thought there must be a defect in one of his eyes, because The Slogger occasionally jumped in a peculiar style, as though he could not see very well. He soon found out, however, there was nothing wrong with his eyes.

The Slogger had a habit of not exactly shirking his fences, but of jumping them sideways in a somewhat slovenly manner This was a defect Dudley Massie hoped to cure by exercising patience. In the stable The Slogger seemed timid when anyone approached his head and attempted to bridle him.

'He must have been hit over the head some time,' thought Dudley, 'or he would not be so nervous at anyone touching him on it.'

At last Dudley Massie came to the conclusion The Slogger had been badly treated, and he put the horse's faults down to the credit of Morgan Sherburn. He knew the former owner of The Slogger was not a man to spare any animal that offended him. He had seen Morgan Sherburn flog a horse unmercifully when the animal was beaten, and had done its best to win. Perhaps The Slogger had experienced some of this treatment, and resented it.

Dudley Massie had plenty of patience, but The Slogger tried it sorely at times. When Massie thought he had got the horse thoroughly to understand him, something would occur to dash his hopes to the ground.

November, with its dull, dreary days, had commenced, and still The Slogger had not profited over-much by his training. At the commencement of the month Morgan Sherburn again came to Sefton House. For the first time for several years the Sefton Brewery Company had not paid a large dividend, and, although the concern was as sound as ever, Sir Gordon knew the drop in the price of shares might easily be misunderstood. Sir Gordon was a rich man, and had a large sum of money invested outside the Sefton Company ; but for the credit of the name he was anxious it should maintain its position in the market.

Morgan Sherburn had noticed the sudden fall in the price of these shares, and he determined to take Sir Gordon's advice, and profit by it if possible. Although a spendthrift, Morgan Sherburn was always glad to make money, in order that he might spend more. Making money with him was purely a selfish matter. Ena Sefton was undoubtedly the great attraction that brought him into the country in November, but he was also desirous of learning what Sir Gordon's opinion was about the Sefton shares. On this point his host made no secret of his opinion that he thought buying Sefton shares at their present price was real good business. Morgan Sherburn thanked him for the hint, and at once wrote to his brokers to buy.

Dudley Massie's father had been affected by the fall in the dividend, and it made a considerable difference to his income. Naturally, he felt anxious, and, although he had great faith in Sir Gordon Sefton, he felt half inclined to sell out. Dudley Massie, however, persuaded him matters were all right, and said he must not trouble himself about them.

Nothing would have pleased Morgan Sherburn better than to purchase Charles Massie's shares at a low price.   It was the kind of trans-action he delighted in ; and, moreover, he had a most unreasonable antipathy to Dudley Massie.

One morning, happening by chance to meet Charles Massie on the Five Oaks Farm, Morgan Sherburn bethought him of the Sefton shares.   He knew Charles Massie held a con-siderable number, and if he could be induced to part with them Dudley Massie would no doubt be annoyed.

He broached the subject, and said he had been buying Sefton shares, but doubted whether the deal was a good one on his part.

' I hear you have been thinking of parting with your shares, Mr. Massie.   If you are still in the same mind, I could no doubt find you a customer,' he said.

' I had thought of selling, but my son advised me to hold on, and Sir Gordon did the same. I'm not so sure, however, that a good price would not tempt me.   I'm not so young as I used to be, and I'd sooner have my bit safe, even if I got less interest for it.'

' Quite right,' said Morgan Sherburn.   ' I have a lot of money lying idle, and if you wish to sell your shares, I will buy them to save you any trouble.'

'It is very good of you, I am sure,' said Charles Massie. 'I'll think the matter over. Sakes alive! what's this?'

The exclamation was caused by The Slogger coming at a tearing pace across the farm, and Dudley Massie vainly trying to hold him in hand.

'It looks very like your son and that brute of a horse I once owned,' said Sherburn. 'I am sorry he bought the horse for Sir Gordon. I know what a beast he is, as I have ridden him myself.'

Charles Massie watched The Slogger coming towards them. There was a high hedge and ditch direct in the course the horse was taking. It was a difficult jump, but one Dudley Massie would have sent The Slogger at without hesitation, had he got him well in hand. Under the present circumstances, when The Slogger had the bit between his teeth, and was taking his own course, Massie knew there was every chance of his coming to grief. He saw his father and Morgan Sherburn watching him, and determined at all costs to get The Slogger over the obstacle if possible.

Horses have wilful ways at times, and The Slogger was no exception. The horse saw what sort of a jump was before him, and went

at it full tilt.   Before Dudley Massie had time
to try and steady him, The Slogger was in the
ditch and Dudley Massie had been thrown
over his head.

Dudley quickly scrambled to his feet, and,
seizing the bridle, pulled The Slogger hard until
he scrambled out.   No horseman likes to come
to grief in a rival's presence, and the smile on
Morgan Sherburn's face did not tend to smooth
down Dudley Massie's temper.

'How did this happen?' asked Charles
Massie.   'Did he bolt with you?   It is lucky
you are not hurt.   Mr. Sherburn was telling
me what a brute the horse is.'

'If he is such a desperate brute, I wonder
at Mr. Sherburn wishing to buy him back
again,' said Dudley.

'I never like parting with a horse in the
manner this one was sold.   There was a muddle
over a selling race, and I lost him.   He bolted
with me on more than one occasion, but I
tamed him at last.   I must let you into the
secret,' he went on, addressing himself to
Dudley Massie; 'you will be able to handle
him better then; or perhaps you could persuade
Sir Gordon to let me have him back.'

This remark made Dudley Massie angry.
When a good rider has been thrown, through

no fault of his own, and a rival stands looking on with a supercilious smile, offering to buy the horse to save further danger, he must be a very peculiarly built man indeed who can take such a proposal calmly.

'Perhaps you let the horse go because you were afraid to ride him,' said Dudley. 'I am not. As for parting with him, Sir Gordon Sefton will not do that if he accepts my advice.'

'I'm not afraid to ride any horse,' said Morgan Sherburn, keeping his temper within bounds—and, to do him justice, he was not. 'A horse like The Slogger is likely to break a man's neck if he is not used to him.'

'I have heard it said when a horse leaves your hands he's not much good to anyone else; but The Slogger is an exception. He was startled, and bolted before I could get him in hand,' he went on, turning to his father 'He'll go all right now, and I will ride him home.'

He remounted The Slogger, who had been quieted down by the spill, and did not seem inclined to indulge in any further freaks.

Morgan Sherburn took good care to relate what he had seen to the Seftons, and the mishap was exaggerated considerably.

'He must be a very bad horse indeed if Dudley cannot ride him,' said Arthur Sefton.

'He is a very bad horse when you do not understand him,' said Morgan Sherburn. 'Perhaps you will let me have him back?' he said to Sir Gordon. 'I know his peculiarities, and have ridden him several times.'

'Massie bought him for me,' said Sir Gordon, 'and I do not care to sell him without consulting him. I will ask him about the matter in the morning.'

'Thanks,' said Sherburn, who was inwardly delighted to think he might possibly get The Slogger back into his possession.

'I am sure Dudley will advise you not to part with him,' said Arthur. 'He is not afraid of any horse, and if The Slogger bolted to-day, you may be sure he will not get another chance of doing so in a hurry.'

When Dudley Massie returned home, and heard from his father that Morgan Sherburn had offered to buy the Sefton shares, he saw at once that it would be a difficult matter to steer clear of his enmity. He strongly urged his father not to sell the shares, and eventually persuaded him to keep them.

'The money will belong to you and Mary,' said his father, 'when I am gone; so if you think it is all right I will make no change.'

'It will be many a long year, I hope, before

we come into the money,' said Dudley Massie. 'We'll not talk about that part of the business. What I want you to do is to take no notice of Morgan Sherburn. He's a bad lot, father, and if he wishes to buy your shares, he has some selfish motive at the bottom of it all. I think it an excellent reason to hold on, when a man like Sherburn wishes to buy.'

Mary Massie was often at Sefton House, and she and her brother always exchanged confidences. She had formed quite as low an opinion of Morgan Sherburn as her brother, and was much surprised at Ena Sefton's preference for his society. She thought her brother admired Ena Sefton, and wished it had been Beatrice he favoured. Ena Sefton was condescendingly polite to Mary Massie, but Beatrice made a friend of her.

She saw her brother after he had the conversation with her father, and they summed Morgan Sherburn's conduct up accurately.

'I think he admires Ena Sefton,' said Mary.

Dudley gave a hearty laugh, as he said :

'I dare say he does : it's like his impertinence. But the grapes are very sour. Fancy Miss Sefton suffering such a man's admiration ! It is too ridiculous, Mary, and the mere mention of it amuses me.'

'He is a very rich man,' said Mary, 'and Ena Sefton is fond of money.'

'You are prejudiced against her,' he said; 'Beatrice is your friend. You never cared for Miss Sefton.'

'I admire her beauty, and I think her a very grand lady,' said Mary, 'but for a friend I certainly prefer Beatrice.'

Dudley Massie was silent for some time, thinking over what his sister had said. He knew there was not much chance of Ena Sefton regarding him as more than a mere acquaintance, but he could not bring himself to think she would ever choose a man like Morgan Sherburn. The mere thought irritated him, and he was vexed with his sister for even hinting at such a thing.

Mary Massie, however, did not regard Ena Sefton through such glowing spectacles as her brother, and she had an idea that millions would weigh heavily in the balance with her.

CHAPTER VI.

A MEETING OF THE TALENT.

PARK LANE is hardly the place to expect to find a meeting of 'the talent' held. Strange men are, however, to be found in strange places, and there is no telling what a wealthy young man will do, even in a house in Park Lane.

Morgan Sherburn patronized several members of the ring, not the betting ring, but the fighting arena, where, for a consideration, certain men battered each other to amuse the public and earn money for themselves.

The ring is a different thing at the present day from what it was in years gone by, when men fought for the championship in a fair and honourable way, and used their bare fists in the encounter. In the days of Tom Sayers the patrons of the ring were men of position, holding offices of State, and noblemen, who scorned anything unfair. When the ring was pitched in a field, and the fighters battled for small stakes and much glory, the practice of the 'noble art' was very different to what it is in these times.

The class of men Morgan Sherburn patronized was not calculated to raise the ring from the depths of degradation into which it had fallen. There were, however, one or two men well up in the 'noble art' who fought fairly, and did their level best to win on their merits. These men fought shy of Morgan Sherburn's protégés, although in the ring they were always ready to meet and beat them if possible.

Morgan Sherburn was 'at home' in his splendid house in Park Lane to several pugilists of doubtful reputation. One of the first men to arrive was a big, burly, coarse-looking man, nearly six feet high, and a desperate customer to tackle from all appearances. He was quietly dressed in a dark suit, and had a blue tie, in which was stuck a pin with the representation of two men sparring in a ring on it. The man drove up in a hansom, and, when he had paid the driver, rang the bell in such a manner that there could be no doubt he did not desire to be kept waiting. The footman who opened the door gave him a condescending glance, not unmixed with a certain amount of admiration. The man had a weakness for the members of the ring, and knew the big fellow's reputation as a fighter stood high.

'Governor at home?' said the caller, in a heavy voice.

'Mr. Sherburn is upstairs in his room. I will announce you,' said the footman.

'All right, get on ahead,' said the man.

The footman preceded him upstairs, and, throwing open the door, said :

'Michael Malone wishes to see you.'

'Send him in,' replied Sherburn. 'So you're here first, Mick,' he added, as the man came in and sat down.

Although the fellow was very much out of harmony with his surroundings, he did not seem ill at ease, but coolly surveyed the room and its occupant.

'When will the others be here?' he asked.

'In about an hour,' said Morgan Sherburn. 'I wanted to have a talk with you alone; that is why I asked you to come earlier.'

'What's on?' asked Malone.

'Dusky Jim is on, or wants to be on,' said Sherburn. 'Are you disposed to give him a chance?' and he looked hard at the man.

A fierce look, half defiance and half hesitation, crossed the man's face. He did not reply at once, and Sherburn said :

'If you do not care to tackle him, I'll try Abe Steel; but I thought I would give you first chance, and I wanted to hear what you had to say, so that when Steel came I could tell him the matter was as good as arranged.'

'Who says I don't care to tackle him?' said Mick Malone fiercely. 'He's only a beastly nigger!'

'Never mind his colour; you fellows generally fall back on the colour excuse when you are afraid,' said Sherburn.

'There's no man dare say I'm afraid to meet him,' said Mick.

'Oh yes there is!' said Sherburn. 'If you decline the engagement, I shall say it.'

Mick Malone glared at Morgan Sherburn savagely, but he merely laughed. Morgan Sherburn loved to play with these big strong fellows, and tease them much in the same manner as he would have done a caged tiger. It was a dangerous process, but the element of danger in it made it more attractive. Mick Malone could have smashed Morgan Sherburn, in such a manner that his friends would not have known him, with the greatest ease, but he refrained from doing so for various reasons. Morgan Sherburn was a liberal patron, and always paid his men well, win or lose.

'Why do you not care to meet this fellow?' said Sherburn; 'I am sure you would beat him.'

'Perhaps I should, but I have a kind of presentiment Dusky Jim would be too much for me. Do you know, I have dreamt three times that black chap will be the death of me.'

The man looked and spoke in such a solemn manner that Morgan Sherburn burst out laughing.

'Don't laugh at me like that, curse you!' said Malone. 'You may not believe what I say, but it's true.'

Mick Malone was a superstitious man. He had been reared in a hotbed of superstition and priestly fallacies. He firmly believed in his dream, and therefore his courage was the greater when he said :

'I'll fight Dusky Jim. You may reckon on me for that. How much are the stakes? Who is backing the black-fellow?'

'Pearce Holden backs him, and the stakes are for a thousand a side, at the Fistic Club. You are in pretty good trim, but the match will not take place before February or March, so you will have ample time to get fit. I am glad you have accepted. I had much rather back you than Abe Steel,' said Morgan Sherburn. 'Mind you don't dream any more ridiculous things—about being killed, and so on. Only fools believe in dreams. I expect Abe

Steel will be mad when he finds you have got the job. I shall say it was a case of first come, first served, and that as you arrived first you got the chance. Steel can tackle you if you win.'

'I'd like to see him,' said Mick Malone. 'I guess I'd have an easier job to beat Abe than I shall have with Dusky Jim.'

Abe Steel, accompanied by two other men of a similar stamp, duly arrived. Steel had won several battles, and was known amongst the fancy as 'the Birmingham Pet.' When he heard that Mick Malone had received the first offer to fight Dusky Jim for two thousand pounds, he wished to settle which was the better man, himself or Mick Malone, on the spot.

Nothing would have pleased Morgan Sherburn better than an impromptu affair of this kind, but he thought of the damage his property might sustain in the course of the encounter.

The men were on their feet squaring at each other, when Morgan Sherburn said :

'Sit down, you fools! I won't have any disturbance here. If Mick wins you can make a match with him afterwards, Steel.'

'Him win!' said Abe Steel. 'I'd like to see him at it! Dusky Jim will wipe the floor with him. You'll lose your money, and serve you right!'

Mick Malone sprang to his feet and caught Abe Steel by the throat.

'Wipe the floor, is it, you dirty Brummagem heathen!' howled Mick; 'I'll show you how to wipe floors!'

The brawny Irishman was in a fury, and he had taken Abe Steel somewhat unawares. Exerting all his strength, he pushed Abe Steel backwards until he crashed into a table on which stood several racing cups under glass cases. There was a tremendous smash, and Abe Steel fell on his back amidst the débris, with Mick Malone on the top of him.

Morgan Sherburn seized a heavy hunting-crop, and commenced to belabour Malone fiercely. He called to the other two men to assist him.

It was, however, a difficult matter to separate the two men. Abe Steel was thoroughly roused, and the fighting instinct in him had the upper hand. They were struggling desperately on the floor, until, by sheer force, Sherburn and the two men dragged Malone off Steel. The difficulty then was to calm Abe Steel and keep him from flying at Mick Malone.

It took some time to pacify the two men, and they sat glaring at each other like wild beasts. A word or two would have set them at each other's throats again, despite their surroundings.

' You brutes !' said Sherburn. ' Look what you have done. Hanging is too good for such fellows !'

' He'd no business to get on to me like he did,' commenced Malone ; but Morgan Sherburn stopped him and said

' I don't want to hear another word. You clear out, Steel. I wish to arrange with Mick about the fight.'

Abe Steel grumbled and went to the sideboard, upon which stood a liqueur-stand. He poured out some brandy, and, uncorking a soda, mixed himself a drink. As he left the room he said :

' You'll be sorry you pitched upon Malone for this match. The black - fellow will kill him.'

Mick Malone rushed towards the door, but Morgan Sherburn was too quick for him. He pushed Steel out, and then locked the door.

' Sit down,' he said to the irate Mick ; ' you have done enough damage for one day. Look at that mess on the floor. I put more store by

5

one of those cups than I do by half a dozen such men as you and Steel. I shall begin to be sorry I ever dirtied my hands with you.'

'There was plenty of dirt on your hands before I met you,' said Mick Malone. 'Some of those cups you set so much store by were not very cleanly won, by all accounts.'

Morgan Sherburn looked hard at Malone, and said

'If you dare to speak to me like that again, I'll throw you over and make this match with Abe Steel.'

Mick Malone calmed down at this, for he knew Morgan Sherburn had a will of his own, and would probably do as he said.

'It wasn't my fault,' said Mick.

'We'll drop the subject, and come to business,' said Sherburn. 'Where are you going to train?'

'At my brother's place, at Putney,' said Mick.

'I think you had better go farther away,' said Sherburn. 'If you go to Putney, Abe Steel will always be down there, and, after to-day, he will not be very amiable. It does not matter to me if you batter each other to pieces, only you must wait until this fight is over. I know a place near Windsor where you can go, and Abe Steel will not trouble to go there.'

' It don't matter much to me where it is,' said Mick ; ' I can get fit anywhere this winter.'

' Then, meet me at the *Sportsman* office, and we'll fix up the match next week,' said Morgan Sherburn. ' I have nothing more to say to you now, so you can go. Remember one thing : if you do anything to prejudice your chance in this fight, I shall not pay you six-pence, and will never have any further dealings with you.'

Mick Malone nodded, and when he left, the other two men, who had taken but little part in the proceedings, followed him.

' What a relief !' said Morgan Sherburn, when they were gone. ' They have made me thirsty. I think I'll have a bottle of champagne. No good wasting such wine on them. Bah ! what beasts they are ! But that fellow Malone is the best of them, and has plenty of pluck. He ought to beat Dusky Jim. Let me see. Dud-ley Massie is a great friend of Pearce Holden's, and no doubt he'll back the black-fellow. I should like to win a few hundreds from him. He does not often bet heavily, but perhaps I can find out a way to induce him to do so. I must think it over.'

CHAPTER VII.

CHRISTMAS IN THE COUNTRY.

IT was a severe winter, and Dudley Massie had hard work to keep The Slogger and other of Sir Gordon's horses in work. Hunting had been out of the question for several weeks, and there did not appear to be much chance of a break-up of the frost, judging from the outlook. Winter was always a trying time to Arthur Sefton, as he could not stand the cold, and therefore had to remain indoors. The Seftons had a large house-party for Christmas, and amongst those who accepted invitations were Morgan Sherburn, Fred Lostock, and Pearce Holden, with whom Sherburn had made the match between Mick Malone and Dusky Jim. Several ladies were of the party, and altogether they had a jolly time, despite the fact that there was no hunting.

In the grounds at Sefton House was a large lake, and the ice was kept in splendid condition for skating ; this formed the chief outdoor amusement, and the invigorating pastime was thoroughly enjoyed. It was an animated scene on the lake the week after Christmas, when several people from the village of Ollerton, and also from the houses round, were present.

Ena Sefton was a graceful and skilful skater, and Morgan Sherburn became more and more infatuated with her as he saw her dressed in handsome furs and in close-fitting costume that suited her figure admirably. He paid her much attention, and she allowed him to monopolize her more than on any previous occasion.

Sir Gordon Sefton could not shut his eyes any longer to the fact that Morgan Sherburn admired Ena, and that she encouraged him. Morgan Sherburn was not the man Sir Gordon would have chosen for his daughter Ena; but he was accustomed to give way to his wife in such matters, and Lady Sefton had at last emphatically declared in favour of this suitor for Ena's hand.

'I thought you wished Ena to marry a title,' said Sir Gordon. 'Morgan Sherburn is a very rich man, but I doubt if he will make a good husband, and he is not at all likely to secure a title.'

'There I differ from you, Gordon,' replied his wife. 'Morgan Sherburn's wealth will secure him a title in time if he goes the proper way about it. Money is a sure road to a title nowadays—more's the pity. Mere merit has very little to do with it. Titles are bought quite as freely now as in days gone by, only the purchase-money is expended in a different manner.'

Sir Gordon laughed as he said :

'Probably you are right. We see big bids for titles made every year; but I doubt if Morgan Sherburn would throw much cash away on a title.

'If he marries Ena, you may trust her to lead him in the right direction. Ena has a masterful way of her own, and she generally secures what she wants,' said Lady Sefton.

'Do you like Morgan Sherburn ?' asked Sir Gordon, looking at her curiously.

Lady Sefton did not meet his gaze, but she replied :

'He is a very rich man, and I can trust Ena to take care of herself.'

Sir Gordon sighed as he said :

'I am afraid we cannot call it a love match if Morgan Sherburn proposes to her. However, if Ena accepts him I shall not withhold my consent.' Then he thought : 'I am glad it is not Beatrice. Neglect would make her miserable ; but Ena is too proud and self-reliant to make trouble where it can be avoided.'

Fred Lostock's income was not what it ought to be—so he said—although he had ample means for a bachelor. He was a favourite with the ladies, and they generally treated him as a friend and comrade. Bachelor Fred, as he was sometimes called, always managed to have a good time in the country houses where he was a welcome guest. If there were junior members of the family to be amused, Fred Lostock was the man to be relied upon. It was no uncommon thing, when Bachelor Fred was missing, on a search being instituted for him, to discover him in the children's quarters, where he was amusing the young ones vastly. Fred Lostock was a peculiar mixture of a man-about-town, who was not given over entirely to the sins of the city, but revelled in the innocent amusements of youth. Mothers were never afraid of trusting their children with Fred Lostock.

During his stay at the Seftons', Fred Lostock had watched with no small degree of curiosity the ' comedy of courtship ' being enacted before him. He prided himself on being a man of discernment, but he failed to understand what attraction Ena Sefton found in Morgan Sherburn. He thought he understood Sherburn's tactics, and was not surprised at his admiration

for Ena Sefton.   He had made great friends
with Dudley Massie, and discovered that young
man, if not in love with Ena, was in a fair way
to become so.   He wished, for Massie's sake,
that matters would turn out all right, but he
did not expect them to do so.

'The haughty Ena,' he thought, 'would
never condescend to regard my friend Dudley
Massie as a suitable man to marry.   He's worth
a dozen such men as Morgan Sherburn.   But
that is the perversity of women.   They are, as
a rule, bad judges of men ; if Ena Sefton knew
half as much about Morgan Sherburn as I do
she would barely speak to him.   It's not my
business to enlighten her, but I certainly think,
if Sherburn wants to marry her, Sir Gordon
ought to forbid the sacrifice.'

He ruminated in this strain as he watched
Ena Sefton and Morgan Sherburn skating
together on the lake.   It was an animated scene.
There could not have been less than a hundred
people on the lake, most of them good skaters,
and revelling in the exercise which the sharp
frosty air made the more enjoyable.   Dudley
Massie was skating with Miss Maud Lance,
the daughter of a neighbouring farmer, and a
very pretty girl.   She skated well, but Dudley
Massie did not seem to be a very amusing

companion. He was dull, and lacked conversation, which was unusual for him. Miss Lance could not fail to notice his abstraction, and after several attempts to rouse him, she gave up the task in despair and said she would rest awhile.

Fred Lostock came to her as she sat in a chair close to the edge of the ice, and thought, as he looked at her glowing healthy face, what a pretty girl she was. He mentally contrasted her complexion with that of Marie de Tourville, whom he had met at Morgan Sherburn's a night or two before they came down to Sefton House.

'Have you deserted Mr. Massie?' he said. 'I am sorry for him.'

'He has deserted me,' said Miss Lance, smiling as she glanced at her questioner. 'I never knew him to be so dull. Is he in love, or has The Slogger gone lame?'

'Does love cause people to be dull?' said Fred. 'I can quite understand his conversation being a shade incoherent if The Slogger is lame.'

'Never having been in love myself, I cannot describe the sensation,' said Maud Lance. 'I suppose it is useless to ask a confirmed bachelor like you if he has ever been in that state?'

'I am always in love,' said Fred. 'I adore

beautiful objects, dead or alive, and therefore I am always in a state of bliss when young ladies such as Miss Maud Lance deign to shine upon me.'

'Compliments from you, Mr. Lostock, are acceptable,' said Miss Lance. 'We always know you mean what you say.'

'Thank you,' said Fred. 'May I have the pleasure of a turn on the ice with you ?'

Miss Lance accepted with alacrity, and they were quickly gliding amongst the skaters.

'Mr. Sherburn is very attentive to Miss Sefton,' said Maud Lance.

'Very,' replied Fred ; 'but that is only natural, as she is the daughter of his host and hostess.'

'You know what I mean very well,' said Miss Lance.

'Do I ? Of course I do : you mean what you say,' replied Fred.

'How provoking you are ! I mean Mr. Sherburn is evidently in love with Miss Sefton.'

'Upon my word ! now you mention it, I have noticed he is attracted by her,' replied Fred.

'What sort of a man is Mr. Sherburn?' asked Miss Lance.

'He is a man of many millions,' said Fred. 'I wish he would hand an odd million or two over to me.'

'Really, Mr. Lostock, how very dense you are this morning! I know Mr. Sherburn is a millionaire. I mean, what sort of a moral character does he bear?' said this persistent young lady.

'Mr. Sherburn's morality is beyond me,' replied Fred. 'Millionaires have a moral code of their own. Not being within miles of a millionaire, I cannot decipher the code.'

'Is Mr. Sherburn a very good young man?' she asked, her eyes sparkling with merriment.

'An excellent young man,' said Fred. 'His generosity is unbounded.'

'I heard he lavished presents upon his *friends* with a free hand,' said Miss Lance.

'Ah,' said Fred, 'I am afraid someone has been telling tales out of school, and you have heard them.'

'Oh look, Mr. Lostock!' exclaimed Miss Lance; 'Miss Sefton and Mr. Sherburn are far too near that broken ice. They must be very much occupied with each other.'

Ena Sefton and Morgan Sherburn were very much occupied. They had been skating together for a considerable time, and Morgan

Sherburn had at last made up his mind to ask Ena Sefton to marry him. He was leading up to this point as skilfully as he knew how, and Ena Sefton, knowing what was coming, felt this was a crisis in her life.

So full of thoughts were they that they glided quickly along the ice, and failed to notice their approach to the spot where the ice had been broken and a danger notice posted.

Dudley Massie saw them, and his cry of warning caused Ena Sefton to look ahead. She saw the danger at once, and quickly released her hands from Morgan Sherburn's grasp.

'Separate,' she said, 'or the ice will break.' She was quite cool and collected.

Morgan Sherburn turned quickly to the left, and Ena went to the right, but, unfortunately, one of her skates caught in a crack in the ice and she fell heavily. The ice beneath her gave way, and in a moment she was in the water. It was so intensely cold that it seemed to numb her, but she did not lose her presence of mind.

Dudley Massie saw what was likely to happen before the ice broke, and skated rapidly to the spot. He lay down flat on the ice and stretched out his hands to Ena Sefton, who was holding herself up as best she could.

'Take hold of my hands,' he said ; 'and I shall be able to support you.'

Ena Sefton loosened her hold of the ice, and clutched Dudley Massie's hand ; but as she did so, the ice again broke, and he was precipitated into the water.

He caught Ena Sefton round the waist with one arm, and put his other on the edge of the ice.

Meanwhile, men with ropes were at hand, and they quickly threw the looped end to Dudley Massie. He seized it and passed it round Ena's waist, and she was dragged on to the ice out of danger. Dudley Massie waited until another rope was thrown, and then he pulled himself out of the water. Morgan Sherburn watched this episode with strange feelings. He wished he had been in Dudley Massie's place. True, the danger was not great, but he thought it would have made a favourable impression upon Ena had he been able to assist her. Whatever credit attached to the affair would now be given to Dudley Massie.

Ena Sefton at once proceeded home with her father, and Dudley Massie sped across the fields at a brisk run to Five Oaks Farm.

Ena Sefton had not spoken a word to him

when he was assisting her in the water, but she gave him a glance that made his pulses tingle when she was safe on the ice again. As for Ena, when she had changed her clothes she felt quite herself again.

'I must thank him for his plucky conduct,' she said to herself. 'What a fine, strong man he is!'

Then she dismissed Dudley Massie from her thoughts and said:

'It happened at an unfortunate moment. Mr. Sherburn would have proposed to me in another minute or two, and I should have answered him. When he does ask me to be his wife, what shall I say?'

She thought for some moments, and then said:

'Wealth means power, and I love power. If I marry you, Morgan Sherburn, you will have to make me a rich woman in my own right.'

———

CHAPTER VIII.

ENA SEFTON'S DECISION.

MORGAN SHERBURN determined to bring matters to a climax with Ena Sefton. He soon found an opportunity. After dinner he waited until he saw her pass into the conservatory, and then quickly followed her.

' I hope you feel no ill effects from your cold bath,' he commenced.

' No,' she replied. ' It was rather invigorating, and, thanks to Mr. Massie, there was very little danger. I have no doubt I looked rather ridiculous when I landed on the ice again. It is certainly not dignified to be dragged out of the water by a rope.'

' Mr. Massie was a lucky man to have such an opportunity afforded him. I envied him immensely,' said Morgan Sherburn.

' His position was not an enviable one,' she replied, ' but he was very useful, and I must thank him for his assistance.'

' He will hardly expect to be thanked for such a trifle,' said Sherburn.

' Trifle it may have been,' said Ena, ' but, nevertheless, the trifle was valuable, and I should be ungrateful not to thank him for acting as he did. He is a fine young fellow, do you not think so ?'

Dudley Massie compared with Morgan Sherburn more than favourably, and the latter knew it.

' Smart sort of fellow for a farmer's son,' he replied. ' I do not suppose he has seen much of the world, and, therefore, one cannot expect him to have much polish.'

'Some people are too highly polished,' said Ena. ' They are polished to such an extent that their characters are reflected upon the shining surface.'

' You are inclined to be sarcastic,' he said. ' Miss Sefton,' he added in a changed tone of voice, ' I did not follow you here to talk about Mr. Massie. He does not concern me at all. I want to talk about yourself.'

' And what have you to say about me that I should care to hear ?' she asked.

' You must have seen that I have admired you for some time, ever since I first met you. That admiration has developed into a deeper feeling, and I can now say truthfully I love you. I am a man of few words, Miss Sefton, but I hope, if you will honour me by becoming my wife, my actions will speak louder than mere words. Will you be my wife, Miss

Sefton—Ena ? I am, as you are aware, a rich man. You have been accustomed to luxuries, and as my wife, I think I may venture to say you will be able to gratify your tastes, however expensive they may be. Again I ask you, will you be my wife and make me the happiest of men ?'

The proposal was made, and Ena Sefton had to decide what her future life should be. Now she had the chance of becoming Morgan Sherburn's wife, she hesitated. She did not intend to refuse his offer, but in the few brief moments in which she remained silent after his proposal a world of thoughts flashed across her mind. She remembered all she had heard about Morgan Sherburn's character, and she called to mind some of his more noted escapades. She gave a slight shiver of aversion.

Morgan Sherburn noticed it, and thought she had caught a chill. He at once became solicitous on her behalf.

She received his attentions without comment, and he thought it best to give her time to answer him. He had not long to wait. Ena Sefton raised her head and looked at him proudly, almost defiantly, as though challenging him in all she was about to say. She was

6

taller than Morgan Sherburn, and as he stood before her, he looked like a jockey in evening dress about to receive instructions from his employer Some such thought as this crossed Ena's mind, and she smiled faintly. She said to him :

'You have asked me to be your wife, Mr. Sherburn, and I am not insensible of the value of your offer ; I may also say it is not un-expected, because I do not pretend to have failed to notice the preference you showed for my society. You say you have always admired, and now you love me. I doubt if you are deeply in love with me, but I am glad you admire me. When a man admires any-thing, he generally cares for the object of his admiration, and is solicitous for its well-being. I think there is more admiration than love in your feelings for me. You wish to feel also the pride of possession, of possessing myself. We must thoroughly understand each other, and then there will be no cause for recrimination afterwards. I cannot say I love you, but I am sure, if you treat me with the respect due to me, I can make you a good wife, and a wife you will be proud of. This is, I think, what you desire, and, having asked me to be your wife, I conclude I shall fulfil that desire. You are a very rich man, and you weigh your wealth in the scale against any personal attraction I may possess. I am not insensible to the value of your wealth, and I shall not play the hypocrite and pretend that without your wealth I should consider your proposal in the same light as I now do. I am speaking plainly before I give you my answer. If after what you have heard you wish to withdraw your proposal, please do so.'

Morgan Sherburn knew she had summed up the situation accurately, and he was a little bit afraid of her. She had hinted at many things he fancied might have been hidden from her.

'After hearing what you have said, I am more than ever desirous you should become my wife. You may have heard rumours about me that are incorrect. I do not profess to be a saint or even a good young man who has never gone wrong in his life. If you become my wife, you will be treated with the respect due to you and which you have a right to exact. Again I ask, will you be my wife?'

'Yes,' she replied.

He took her hand, but there was no lovers' fervent embrace. They seemed to have made a compact of a worldly nature, in which love

was considered an unimportant factor. Such
marriages are often made, but the contracting
parties have not always the honesty to confess
the motives actuating them.

'I am very glad and proud you have consented to become my wife,' he said. 'You
shall never have cause to regret the step you
have taken. I must consult with your father
as to your settlement, for I wish you to have
what many people would consider a fortune, in
your own right.'

He said this in a business-like way that
rather jarred upon Ena Sefton's proud nature.
She had heard he was lavish in making
presents, and this offer of a settlement sounded
rather similar. She made up her mind the
settlement should be a handsome one.

'My father will of course arrange such
matters with you,' she replied. 'Please do not
forget I am rather extravagant, and shall not
care to trouble you about money matters more
than I can possibly help. You had better
speak to Sir Gordon as soon as possible.'

'I will,' he replied. 'You have made me
very happy,' he said, drawing closer to her.
He was inclined to become affectionate, but her
look checked him, and he did not like it. He
thought : 'Wait until we are married, my

haughty thoroughbred. You'll pull too hard in a snaffle—I shall have to put on the curb.'

' I will leave you now,' said Ena. 'We have been here for some time, and our absence will be noticed. Here is my father coming this way. It is a lucky chance. You can speak to him now.'

She advanced to meet Sir Gordon, and said :

' Mr. Sherburn wishes to speak to you. I have accepted him. He proposes to be generous as to settlements.'

A curiously worldly speech for a daughter to make to her father a few minutes after promising to be a wife !

Sir Gordon started. He was not surprised at Morgan Sherburn proposing to Ena, but he was surprised at the way in which she spoke of it. Before he had time to reply Ena left him, and he walked into the conservatory and joined Morgan Sherburn.

' You have heard the news ?' he said to Sir Gordon. ' Miss Sefton has honoured me by accepting me as a husband, with your approval. I trust you will give your consent. No doubt you have seen I admired Ena ?'

' I cannot say I have not noticed your partiality for her society,' said Sir Gordon ; ' but this is rather sudden. Are you quite sure you understand your feelings towards each other?'

'Perfectly,' replied Morgan Sherburn; 'we understand each other admirably.'

'Ena is my eldest child,' said Sir Gordon, 'and I wish to see her happiness secured. Are you quite sure you will make her happy?'

'I will do my best, Sir Gordon,' he said; 'Ena is not a woman who places love before all, and we shall be perfectly contented without any maudlin sentimentality for each other. I am willing to make her a handsome settlement, and she wishes it.'

He named the sum he proposed to settle upon Ena, and Sir Gordon opened his eyes. It was a very large amount, and he had not expected it of Morgan Sherburn. Perhaps, after all, he began to think, he had done the man an injustice. Settling such a sum upon Ena was practically making her her own mistress.

'You are very liberal, not to say generous,' Sir Gordon replied. 'It is a good augury for the future.'

'Then you consent to our marriage?' asked Morgan Sherburn.

'Yes,' replied Sir Gordon; 'and I will at once consult Lady Sefton.'

'I should like the marriage to take place soon,' said Sherburn.

'Ladies always require considerable notice on such occasions,' replied Sir Gordon, smiling.

'Say a month,' said Morgan Sherburn, 'and then we shall have got the honeymoon over before the Grand National.'

'You ride in that race?' asked Sir Gordon.

'I hope to do so, if my candidate keeps well. I am sure Ena will not object to a short engagement,' he said.

'I will see what can be done,' replied Sir Gordon. 'If Ena consents, the matter is as good as settled. She generally has her own way.'

They talked for some little time, and then Sir Gordon went in search of Lady Sefton, and found Ena with her.

'I have told mother about our engagement,' said Ena, 'and she approves. Have you given your consent, and arranged as to the settlement?'

'I have,' said Sir Gordon; 'Mr. Sherburn has behaved most generously;' and he named the sum Morgan Sherburn intended to settle upon Ena.

Although Ena Sefton had expected a stiff sum, she had no idea Morgan Sherburn would put such a high value upon her, and she was the more gratified. Morgan Sherburn had judged her rightly. He knew the best passport to Ena's favour was to deal generously towards her. She began to think her future husband must be very fond of her indeed.

Ena Sefton consented to a speedy marriage, although her mother wished for a longer time in which to prepare. Ena, however, overruled her objections.

She thanked Morgan Sherburn for his generosity in such a hearty and friendly manner that he was enchanted with her. She could afford to be kind to him now he had gratified her desire.

'We shall be a model couple,' said Morgan Sherburn, smiling.

'There is ample room for a few models of that description in London society,' quickly replied Ena Sefton.

CHAPTER IX.

AT SEFTON HOUSE STABLES.

THE first time Ena Sefton met Dudley Massie after the accident, she thanked him for his timely aid.

' I was only too pleased to have the chance
of rendering you assistance, however slight,' he
replied. ' I wish it had been a greater service.'

The tone in which he spoke, his look, and
the evident anxiety to please her, struck Ena
Sefton and attracted her attention. A sudden
thought crossed her mind that perhaps Dudley
Massie also admired her. Mentally, she contrasted her accepted lover with the man
standing before her, and Morgan Sherburn
suffered by the comparison.

Ena Sefton had never noticed before what
a really handsome man Dudley Massie was.
She was vexed with herself for noticing it at
this particular time. Her determination to at
once tell him of her engagement was impulsive.

' Mr. Massie,' she said, somewhat abruptly,
' do you know Mr. Sherburn well ?'

It was not what she had intended to say—
far from it ; but the words were spoken before
she thought what the answer might be.

Dudley Massie regarded her curiously for a
few moments, and then said :

' I am not a friend of Mr. Sherburn's. I
certainly know the character he bears on the
race-course and in sporting circles generally,
but that would not interest you.'

' You are mistaken,' she replied : ' everything connected with Morgan Sherburn interests me *now.*'

The stress she placed upon the last word caused him to start, and he turned pale.

' Pardon my curiosity in asking why you are more interested in him now than you were yesterday,' he replied.

' Because I am engaged to him,' she said.

He did not at once reply, and she said impatiently:

' Why do you not answer my question ?'

' I would rather not answer it now,' he replied. ' I wish you had not asked me for my opinion. I did not know you were engaged to him.'

' I do not wish that fact to prevent your answering my question,' she said. ' Has Mr. Sherburn a bad reputation on the turf?'

' He has not a good reputation,' said Dudley Massie.

' I thought as much,' she said ; ' please go on. I am interested.'

' Miss Sefton, I honour and respect you, and I would do much to please you, but I cannot say anything against the man you have chosen for a husband.'

' Why not ?' she said ; ' I take the responsibility of your answer upon myself.'

'There is a reason,' he commenced hesitatingly, 'why I must decline. If you knew that reason you would not press for an answer.'

He had his feelings well under control, but he could not conceal from Ena Sefton what that reason was. Before her engagement to Morgan Sherburn she would have been angry at Dudley Massie's daring to love her; now she felt, though she was annoyed with herself for so feeling, pleased that he did love her.

'I think you are right,' she said slowly, and in a much softer voice than usual. 'I understand what you mean, and, believe me, I honour you for it. Some men would not be so generous.'

After a few commonplace sentences, they parted, and Dudley Massie walked towards the stables in a very dejected frame of mind.

'To think she has selected such a man as Morgan Sherburn for her husband,' he thought. 'She cannot know his true character, and it is not for me to tell her, but she ought to know it in order to be saved the humiliation of marrying such a man. I wonder how much he has told her. Bah! it ought not to trouble me. If she marries him for his money, she must take the consequences.'

When Dudley Massie mounted The Slogger,

and took him for a strong gallop, the horse must have thought his rider was in a peculiar frame of mind.

The Slogger was unaccustomed to rough handling, and it was seldom Dudley Massie so far forgot himself as to pull any horse about.

It so happened that Sir Gordon Sefton and Morgan Sherburn came on to the scene when Dudley Massie was having an argument with The Slogger. Both man and horse were determined. The rider knew he had been in the wrong and provoked the horse's temper, but he also knew that he must not give in to him.

' I am afraid Massie will have some difficulty in training that horse,' said Sir Gordon.

' He does not go the right way about it,' said Morgan Sherburn. ' A horse with such a peculiar temper as The Slogger's requires very careful handling indeed. I think you had better let me have the horse back at the figure you gave for him.'

Sir Gordon laughed, as he replied :

' You are very anxious to buy The Slogger back. I shall think I have a bargain in him if you persist.'

Dudley Massie had at last mastered The Slogger, who at once settled down into his stride, and galloped in fine style.

'He is an excellent mover,' said Sir Gordon.

'Cannot find much fault with him in that line,' said Morgan Sherburn ; 'but it does not matter how good a mover a horse is if he will not do his best in a race, and shows temper at the most critical time.'

'Would you like a spin on him yourself?' asked Sir Gordon.

Morgan Sherburn knew it would be decidedly unpleasant to Dudley Massie if he accepted this offer, and he said :

'I should like to have a ride on him, if he has not had sufficient exercise already.'

Sir Gordon beckoned to Dudley Massie, who rode across to them.

'Mr. Sherburn would like to have a ride on The Slogger, if he has not done too much work this morning,' said Sir Gordon.

Dudley Massie at once saw what Sherburn's move was. He knew if he said The Slogger had already done enough work, Morgan Sherburn would say it was merely an excuse to keep him out of the saddle. If he had a mount on him, he would be able to show off before Sir Gordon, because The Slogger had been quieted down by the recent struggle. Under any circumstances, Dudley Massie did not care for Morgan Sherburn to mount The

Slogger, but he saw no way out of the difficulty, and therefore said he thought it would
do the horse no harm to have another spin.
He dismounted, and handed the reins to
Morgan Sherburn, who was quickly in the
saddle, and sat his horse easily and elegantly,
like the good horseman he undoubtedly was.

'Splendid seat,' said Sir Gordon.

'He has,' replied Massie ; 'but I don't think
his temper is good.'

'The Slogger moves all right with him.'

'Now he does, but I had a hard fight with
him this morning. The more I ride that horse,
the more am I convinced you have a Grand
National winner in him,' said Dudley Massie.

'I hope so,' replied Sir Gordon ; 'I would
sooner win that race than a Derby.'

The Slogger galloped without any trouble,
and Morgan Sherburn, when he dismounted,
felt refreshed.

'He goes well,' he said to Sir Gordon, 'but
his paces are not quite so good as when I had
him.'

Sir Gordon answered him, and then moved
away to converse with the stud-groom, who
had come over from the farm on business.

'You met Miss Sefton this morning ?' asked
Sherburn.

'I did,' replied Dudley Massie.

'Are you aware we are engaged?' asked Sherburn.

'Yes,' replied Dudley. 'She told me.'

'Then, perhaps you will remember I do not choose to have my future wife meeting gentlemen at such early hours, or, in fact, at any hour,' said Sherburn.

'I shall always be happy to either speak to Miss Sefton, or render her any service when she has need of it,' replied Dudley.

'My wife will never have any need of your services, and I do not choose that you should be seen with her before we are married.'

'That must be left entirely to Miss Sefton.' said Dudley. 'If she desires to speak to me, you will certainly not prevent my doing so.'

'I have warned you,' said Sherburn. 'I do not choose that my future wife shall be seen having meetings with her father's servant.'

Morgan Sherburn wished to make Dudley Massie lose his temper, and therefore did not scruple to drag Ena's name into the conversation. Dudley Massie, however, divined his intention, and meant to avoid a quarrel with him in Sir Gordon's presence.

'Miss Sefton is not in the habit of meeting

her father's servants. She would not feel flattered at your remark,' said Dudley.

'She met you this morning,' said Sherburn.

'I am not her father's servant,' said Dudley.

'You ride his horses, and are paid indirectly for your services,' said Sherburn. 'I see very little difference in your position from that of an ordinary servant.'

'I am a gentleman rider,' said Dudley, 'and have never been paid for my services.'

'There is not much to distinguish the gentleman rider from the professional,' said Sherburn.

'In your case, perhaps not,' said Dudley; 'in fact, the professional rider does not lose by comparison.'

'What do you mean to insinuate?' said Sherburn angrily.

'I mean that I have seen you do things in a race that a professional rider would have scorned to be guilty of,' said Dudley.

'That is a lie!' said Sherburn.

Sir Gordon Sefton came up and heard the remark.

'That is strong language,' he said, looking from one man to the other. 'What has given rise to it?'

'Mr. Massie made a serious accusation

against me,' said Sherburn ; 'he accused me of selling races. He may not have used those words, but that is clearly what he meant. It was quite sufficient to warrant the use of a strong expression.'

'I am sorry to hear this,' said Sir Gordon, turning to Dudley Massie. 'Are you aware Mr. Sherburn is engaged to my daughter ?'

Dudley Massie bowed an assent.

'Then how dare you cast aspersions upon Mr. Sherburn's character ?' said Sir Gordon angrily. 'Do you suppose I would entrust my daughter's happiness to anyone but a man of honour ?'

Dudley Massie was still silent.

'Perhaps you do not know he met your daughter alone this morning ?' said Morgan Sherburn.

'I had that honour,' said Dudley Massie. 'Miss Sefton thanked me for the slight service I rendered her when the ice broke.'

'Quite proper,' said Sir Gordon, relieved. 'Come, Sherburn, you are too hasty in drawing conclusions, and you, Massie, ought to be more circumspect in your remarks. I trust, if you have cast any reflection upon Mr. Sherburn's honour, you will withdraw the words.'

'Mr. Sherburn exaggerated what I said,'

7

replied Dudley.   'I did not accuse him of selling races.'

'You implied that I did so,' replied Sherburn·

'Shall I tell Sir Gordon what I know to be true about that race at C——?' asked Dudley.

It was Morgan Sherburn's turn to remain silent, and he tried to laugh the matter off, but succeeded indifferently.

Sir Gordon was ill at ease, and said :

'Such bickerings are most unpleasant. I trust you will both avoid them in the future. Perhaps it must be put down to " professional " jealousy, as you are such good riders.'

Nothing more was said, but the incident rankled unpleasantly in Sir Gordon's mind, for he felt Dudley Massie must have had good grounds for any accusation he had made.

CHAPTER X.

THE GREATER ATTRACTION.

THE wedding had taken place, and Ena Sefton was now Mrs. Morgan Sherburn.   In the excitement of that time, and during the first week of his married life, Morgan Sherburn forgot that the date for the match between Michael Malone and Dusky Jim was at hand.

A letter from Malone's trainer reminded him of
the fact. In this letter the trainer expressed himself as very sanguine of success, and stated that
Malone was trained to the hour. The last few
lines of the epistle, however, annoyed Sherburn
a good deal. The trainer wrote :

'Although, as I have stated, Malone is as
fit as hands can make him, he seems nervous,
and dreads meeting Dusky Jim. He has some
soft idea in his head that the black-fellow will
fatally injure him. I must tell you that Abe
Steel has been here spying out how the land
lies. He met Mick one morning, and I had
the greatest difficulty in preventing their coming
to blows. If Mick Malone loses this fight, it
will be through his own stupidity, and merely
because he has some foolish presentiment about
Jim. I want you to see him as early as
possible and give him a good talking to. Sorry
to disturb you at this particular time, but as the
fight takes place on Tuesday, there should be
no further delay.'

Morgan Sherburn was sitting at the break-
fast-table with his wife, in their private apart-
ments in a hotel in Paris, when he read this
letter, and he gave vent to his feelings in a
rather strong oath. His wife looked at him,
and there was cold contempt in every feature

of her proud, handsome face. Already Ena knew that wealth might be too dearly bought. She calmed her feelings, however, and said :

' I am afraid you have had unpleasant news.'

' Very unpleasant,' he replied. ' I forgot all about an important engagement I made in London for Tuesday next. I may say it was made before our marriage, and I am sorry I cannot cancel it. My presence in London now is absolutely necessary I hope you will not think it very inconvenient to accompany me. Of course, if you prefer to remain here I will return as soon as possible. I am sorry this has happened at such a time.'

' If it is a business engagement, of course it must be attended to,' replied Ena. ' If you do not object, I will remain here until you return.'

' As you wish,' he said. ' Of course I should prefer your society.'

She shrugged her shoulders, and said :

' My dear Morgan, you know very well that is not true. As you have not told me the reason of your sudden departure for London, I can merely guess at it.'

' I told you it was an engagement made before we were married, and that in the pleasure of your society I had forgotten it.'

'If you do not choose to inform me of the nature of the business, I shall not press you to do so,' she replied.

He did not like to tell her he was leaving her to attend a prize-fight.

'I have a considerable sum of money at stake,' he said. 'I made rather a rash wager some months ago, and I think if I go home now I may pull it off.'

'Are you going home to ride in a race?' she asked.

'No,' he replied; and she did not seem relieved at the answer.

'When do you go?'

'By to-night's express.'

'And you return?'

'I can hardly name the day; but it will probably be on Wednesday or Thursday next.'

'Then you will be absent nearly a week?'

'Yes,' he replied, looking at her curiously. He thought she was very anxious to know how long he would be absent.

'Do you think it a proper thing to do, to leave me here after we have been married a little over a week?' she asked.

'It is unavoidable,' he said.

'That is not an answer to my question.'

'Oh, hang it all, Ena! do not be so mighty

particular. Have I not told you it is unavoidable?' he replied.

'If I remain here I shall act exactly as I think proper during your absence,' she said.

'Of course,' he replied; 'and I am sure you will enjoy yourself.'

'Probably,' she said quietly. 'I know how to take care of myself. I trust you do.'

'Rather,' he said, with a vicious smile; 'and I also know how to take care of what belongs to me.'

He rose from the table and went out of the room.

Ena saw he had left the letter on the table, and it was open. Should she read it? She decided in her own interest she ought to do so, but she meant to inform him afterwards of what she had done. She was about to take up the letter when Morgan Sherburn entered. He walked to the table, picked up the letter, and placed it in his pocket.

'Have you read it?' he asked rudely.

'No,' she replied; 'but I should have done so.'

'You are candid,' he sneered.

'I always speak the truth,' she said proudly; 'I thought it my duty to read that letter.'

'Here it is,' he said, drawing it out of his

pocket and throwing it on to the table. 'You can read it with pleasure. There is nothing in it I wish to conceal.'

'You imply that if there were something to conceal, you would not hand it me to read. I conclude from your action you have spoken the truth, and therefore, as there is nothing to conceal in it, I do not care to read it.'

She handed it back to him, and he thrust it angrily into his pocket.

'You are beginning to come the high hand very early in your married life,' he said.

'It is as well to begin as we mean to go on,' she said.

'Quite right. I am glad you have reminded me of that fact ; I ought to have thought of it sooner. A husband has certain privileges, and I mean to have them. Do you understand me ? You are my wife, and you will have to act as such.'

'I shall not give you any cause to complain,' she replied, 'unless you force me to do so.'

For the remainder of the day they did not speak. Before he left he said good-bye to her, and she responded in the same tone.

When he entered the train he felt a feeling of relief.

'She's a regular iceberg,' he thought. 'What a honeymoon !'

Then he commenced to wonder if Marie de Tourville would be so cold. He rather fancied she would be warm—very warm, for he had not seen her since his marriage.

On his arrival in London, he at once drove to Waterloo Station and proceeded to Windsor. He was in a very bad temper, for a long railway journey always irritated him.

When he saw Mick Malone, however, he cooled down. He could not fail to notice the vast improvement that had been made in the man. He complimented the trainer and Malone upon the work that had been done.

'You are certain to win, Mick,' he said.

Mick Malone thrust out a big, long, brawny right arm, with his clenched fist as hard as iron, and the muscles standing out like cords, and said : 'I'd win for certain, but for one thing.'

'And that is ?' asked Sherburn.

'I fear Jim will give me a knock-out blow before I have time to settle him.'

'You're a fool !' said Sherburn. 'Why do you anticipate such bad luck ? If you enter the ring with that sort of feeling in you, you are sure to be beaten. I hear Abe Steel has been here. What has he been up to ?'

' How should I know ?' growled Mick. ' I'd like to fight him with bare knuckles, and find a soft place over his heart.'

' You seem to have a great down on Abe,' said Sherburn.

' I'd like to kill him in a fair fight,' said Mick sullenly, and began to dig away at the punching ball with vicious hits.

' I fancy Abe Steel wronged his sister,' said the trainer.

' Oh,' said Morgan Sherburn, ' I didn't know Mick had such a keen sense of honour.'

' He's more of that stuff in him than you have,' thought the trainer, but wisely said nothing.

Before he returned to London, Morgan Sherburn gave Mick Malone some advice as to the foolish notions he had in his head about Dusky Jim killing him.

' That feeling is not quite so powerful dead against me now,' said Mick ; ' and you can rely upon me to do my best in the ring for you.'

At the Fistic Club the coming fight was the principal subject of conversation. When Morgan Sherburn entered most of the members were surprised to see him, knowing how recently he had been married.

Pearce Holden chaffed him about leaving his

bride, and Fred Lostock wished to know if Mrs. Sherburn had given him permission to attend the fight.

' Of course she returned from Paris with you?' he said. ' I must call and pay my respects.'

' Mrs. Sherburn is in Paris. You could hardly expect her to take much interest in a prize-fight ; besides, I want to have a look round town before I bring her home.'

Dudley Massie had been riding at Sandown, and called in at the Fistic Club when he reached home. Here he met Pearce Holden, who said :

' Who do you think has been here ?'

' I don't know,' said Dudley ; ' was it Jim ? If so, I am sorry I missed him.'

' No, it was not Dusky Jim,' said Holden. ' You will be surprised when you hear.'

' Put me out of suspense.'

' It was Morgan Sherburn.'

Dudley Massie started and said :

'They have not remained away from England very long.'

' Mrs. Sherburn is still in Paris,' said Pearce Holden.

' Do you mean to say he has left her there alone so soon after her marriage ?' asked Dudley.

' That is precisely what I do mean. Sherburn appears to be relieved at her absence, and promises himself a night or two about town before she returns,' said Pearce Holden.

' He's a blackguard,' said Dudley.

' When a woman marries a man like Morgan Sherburn for his money, well knowing his character beforehand, she has very little cause to complain at such treatment,' replied Holden.

' I trust she will prove more than a match for him,' said Fred Lostock, joining in the conversation. ' From what I know of her, I think she is quite capable of holding her own even with Morgan Sherburn.'

Since Ena's marriage Dudley Massie had been more than ever hopelessly in love with her. She exercised a strong power of fascination over him, even when absent. He thought of her in Paris alone. How little Morgan Sherburn knew the prize he had secured! He wondered if Ena knew why Morgan Sherburn had come to London. A prize-fight had far more attraction for this man than a newly-wed and beautiful wife.

' What are you so serious about ?' asked Fred Lostock.

' I was thinking about the coming fight.'

' Dusky Jim will win,' said Fred.

'I hope so,' replied Dudley; 'but I fancy Mick Malone is a trifle too clever for him.'

'Have you anything on?' asked Fred.

'No,' said Dudley; 'but I should like a "pony" on the darkie, just for the pleasure of seeing him beat Sherburn's man.'

'You can have that amount with me,' replied Fred. 'I have bet Sherburn a level hundred on the black-fellow.'

'I hope you will win,' said Dudley, as he booked the wager Fred Lostock laid him.

'Do you think the Seftons know Sherburn is in London and his wife in Paris?' asked Fred.

'No,' replied Dudley; 'but they are sure to hear of it.'

'What on earth made her marry him I can't imagine,' said Fred; 'but the ways of women are beyond me.'

CHAPTER XI.

AT THE FISTIC CLUB.

THE night before the great fight there was a large attendance of members at the Fistic Club, all anxious to gain the latest information about the men. The scene was animated, and it was evident opinions were evenly divided as to the merits of Mick Malone and Dusky Jim. It had been rumoured early in the evening that the two pugilists would appear at the club during the evening, and there was a natural desire to see them, and judge from personal observation as to their fitness.

Dudley Massie dearly loved to see a good fight, when fairly conducted, as such encounters always were under the auspices of the Fistic Club. He decided to remain in town until after the match, and consequently found his way to the club on the evening now named.

He had not been there long before he was joined by Fred Lostock, who was a regular habitué of the place, and was generally brimful of news.

'Anything fresh?' asked Dudley Massie, as Fred came up to him.

'Not much; but I hear Pearce Holden met Sherburn this morning, and laid him another five hundred the black-fellow wins.'

'Holden seems very sanguine,' said Dudley. 'What is your candid opinion about it?'

'I think the darkie will win; but if they come here to-night we shall be better able to form an opinion.'

A stir at the farther end of the room attracted

their attention, and they saw Morgan Sherburn had entered, accompanied by Mick Malone, his trainer, and seconds.

The brawny Irishman received a hearty welcome, for he was popular at the club, and his appearance pleased his numerous backers. Morgan Sherburn, as usual, was patronizing and abrupt to those around him, and there were not many men present who would have shaken him by the hand had he not been a rich man. Sherburn was too conceited to realize this, although he placed full value upon his money. This evening he was irritable and snappish. He was angry with Ena for remaining behind in Paris, and at the same time he was glad she was not in London. He knew she was utterly indifferent about his leaving her alone, and this thought rankled in his mind. A man with such vitiated tastes as Morgan Sherburn seldom credits either women or men with possessing virtues he is himself devoid of. It would have actually pleased Morgan Sherburn to know that his wife was not perfect, and had the failings of her sex fully developed. Had she been such a woman, he would have known how to retaliate, but being what she was, her power was too strong for him.

As he glanced round the room, he saw Dudley Massie. He hated Massie, because he knew the farmer's son would not stoop to do the underhand and contemptible actions he himself thought sharp and clever. Always on the look-out for something to relieve the monotony of his existence, Morgan Sherburn suddenly conceived an idea both base and despicable.

' That's the man who said he would help her if she needed help,' he muttered. ' D—— him and her too! I have half a mind to give him the chance. I should like to humble you, my haughty lady, and if your good name became a little tarnished, you might be more familiar with me. Fancy being married, and no sooner is the ceremony completed than she gives me, her husband, to understand we may be very good friends, but nothing more. That does not suit my book.'

The idea he had in his mind was not fully developed, for he did not act upon the suggestion at once. His attention was taken by the entrance of Dusky Jim. The black-fellow was a fine specimen of an American negro. He was a big powerful man, standing fully six feet, and with an enormous reach. He was quiet and inoffensive, a man not given to seeking quarrels, but rather avoiding them, and in the ring a perfect demon to give and take punishment. He had a good-humoured face, with bright merry eyes. His lips were thick, but not out of keeping with his features, and his nose was well shaped. He was a good-looking black-fellow, with the heart of a white man.

Both Dusky Jim and Mick Malone were popular and respected, because they always fought fairly, and were not given to bragging and boasting of their deeds.

As the two men met in the middle of the room and shook hands, a hearty cheer was given them.

Dusky Jim smiled at Mick Malone, and said :

' However it goes to-morrow night, Mick, I hope we shall always be friends.'

' Sure we shall,' replied Mick. ' I never wish to meet a better man.'

' Nor I,' replied Jim.

The men were nearly the same height, the black man being a shade the taller. Old hands at the game chuckled as they thought what a pair of gladiators they would look when stripped.

Dudley Massie eyed them with feelings of admiration, in much the same manner as he would have scanned The Slogger when fit for a race.

'What a pair!' he said to Fred Lostock. 'They are very evenly matched.'

'Glad you think so,' said Morgan Sherburn. 'I'll bet you a "monkey" my man wins—or, perhaps, a tenner is more in your line.'

The tone was insulting, and Dudley Massie did a very foolish thing. Instead of ignoring Sherburn's remark, he turned on him angrily, and said :

'If you prefer the larger bet, I am willing to take it.'

'I'll book it,' said Morgan Sherburn. 'If you win, it will come in handy for you to make a present to the fair lady you have honoured with your affections.'

Dudley Massie knew what he meant, but he could make no reply without compromising Morgan Sherburn's wife.

'What did he mean?' asked Fred Lostock, as Morgan Sherburn moved away. 'Insulting little beast ; but what can a fellow do with a man like that? You were foolish to take that wager, old chap. Five hundred is a mere nothing to him, but I expect it is to you.'

'I was a fool to accept his challenge,' said Dudley ; 'but now the wager is made I must

8

hope for the best.   As for his insinuation, I do not know what he means, or to whom he alludes.'

Fred Lostock thought to himself, 'Surely Sherburn cannot mean his wife.   Massie was certainly very much attached to her, but she never encouraged him.   I wonder what Morgan's little game is.   He's deep and he's treacherous, and he hates Dudley Massie, but he's not blackguard enough to try and couple their names together.   I like Massie, and, hang me! if he loses that wager I'll help him out, always providing he is not too proud to accept my assistance.'

Many heavy wagers were made that night on the Malone and Coonan fight, and the two men had a friendly bet between themselves for a modest amount.   They laughed and chatted together for over an hour, and no one, to look at them, would imagine they were engaged to fight fiercely the next night.

When the club closed for the night, slight odds were laid on Mick Malone, owing to the amount of money that had been wagered on him.

When he reached home, Morgan Sherburn had a long talk with his valet, Raymond Daly.

This Raymond Daly was a man in every

way suited to his master, so long as that master paid him liberally to keep silent. Raymond Daly was utterly unscrupulous. His one object in life was to make money. He had no compunction whatever in robbing his master when there was no fear of detection, but he had the one merit, if it can be so called, of keeping his master's secrets when well paid for it.

'You must leave Victoria at nine in the morning,' said Morgan Sherburn, 'and you will arrive in Paris at five.'

'Yes, sir.'

'Send that wire at once to Dudley Massie, Fistic Club.'

'Yes, sir.'

'Read its contents.'

Daly took the paper, read what Morgan Sherburn had written, looked at his master and smiled faintly.

' Do you understand it?'

'I can read what you have written.'

'And you do not understand it?'

'No, sir.'

'And you will continue to not understand it. You will obliterate it from that excellent washing tablet of your memory. You will wipe it off the slate, Daly You will also forget you went to Paris on the morning of the great fight. I exceedingly regret you will miss that fight, Daly, because I know you think my man will win.'

' I do, sir. It is a cert for Mick,' said Daly.

' A what ?' asked Sherburn.

' A certainty, sir. I beg your pardon.'

' You must keep up appearances,' said Morgan Sherburn. ' But to recompense you for missing the fight, I have put you a hundred at evens on Malone. Do you understand me ?'

' Yes, sir.'

' And you are perfectly satisfied ?'

' I am always satisfied with your treatment,' said Daly.

' Very good,' replied Sherburn. ' When you are not satisfied with me, Daly, I hope you will remember I know you very well and can give you an excellent character for——'

' Honesty, sir.'

' Sobriety, I was about to say.' replied Morgan Sherburn. ' You will return to London by the 9 p.m. from Paris. You will have four hours in that gay city. To occupy your time you can think over the fight at the Fistic Club and hope you will win your money.'

Next morning, punctually to time, Raymond Daly was at Victoria Station. He left by the nine o'clock train for Paris, and arrived there shortly after five. Having despatched his telegram, he waited patiently for the return train at 9 p.m. Morgan Sherburn seemed in a good humour on the morning of the fight. He went for a ride and returned home for luncheon.

Raymond Daly's absence from the house was hardly noticed, because the man went on so many missions for his master.

Dudley Massie was not in an enviable frame of mind. A sense of impending trouble seemed to hang over him, and he could not shake off the feeling. He wondered what Ena Sherburn was doing in Paris and what had caused her to remain behind instead of accompanying her husband to London. It was no business of his, but he could not help taking an interest in her.

Then there was the wager he had made. He could pay if he lost, that was one comfort, but he would miss the money. He did not bet heavily, and as a gentleman rider he was as often as not out of pocket when he had a mount. He rode for pure love of the sport, and would have scorned to accept bribes and make bargains, as he knew other men did.

He made up his mind he would go back to Five Oaks as soon as the fight was over, and not leave again until just before the National, unless Sir Gordon decided to run The Slogger at Derby.   Gradually he shook off the feeling of oppression, and as he walked to the Fistic Club he felt quite light-hearted and in excellent spirits.

CHAPTER XII.

THE GREAT FIGHT

IF the Fistic Club presented a busy scene the night before the great fight, its then appearance was a mere nothing compared to the evening of that important event.   Every seat around the ring was occupied, high prices being paid for the privilege of seeing these two trained athletes attempt to batter each other's features out of shape.

Morgan Sherburn arrived early, and so did Dudley Massie, who occupied a seat next to Fred Lostock.

The fight was timed to commence at nine o'clock, but it was an understood thing that it would be nearer ten before the men entered the ring.

Dudley Massie had only occupied his seat a few minutes and was talking to Fred Lostock, when an attendant handed him a telegram, saying

'This arrived some time ago, Mr. Massie, but we knew you were coming to-night, so thought it better to keep it until you arrived.'

'Quite right,' replied Dudley. 'Another mount, perhaps,' he added to Fred Lostock as he tore open the envelope.

Fred Lostock soon saw it was not the mere offer of a mount that the telegram contained, for Dudley Massie was strangely agitated, and the hand that held the telegram trembled visibly.

'What's the matter?' said Fred. 'No bad news from home, I trust.'

'They are all well at home, thanks,' said Dudley, ' but this wire is of the utmost import-ance. I am afraid it will cause me to miss the fight.'

' By Jove !' exclaimed Fred, 'it must be serious, then. Can I be of any assistance ? I will do anything short of missing the fight.'

Dudley Massie smiled faintly as he replied :

' Excuse me, Fred. If I dared tell you what this means, believe me, I would do so, but it is better for me to remain silent. If anyone asks for me, say I have been called home suddenly on important business.'

'All right,' said Fred, 'but I am awfully sorry you are going. Try and get out of it if you can. Send a wire and beg off. This will be the most glorious mill we have ever seen at the club, and that is saying a lot.'

As Dudley Massie left the room, Morgan Sherburn watched him with a vindictive look in his eye.

Fred Lostock saw the expression on Morgan Sherburn's face, and it suddenly struck him he might have had a hand in Dudley Massie's sudden departure.

'It would please Sherburn immensely,' thought Fred, 'if he could make Dudley Massie miss the fight. I wonder if that telegram was genuine.'

When Dudley Massie was in the hansom, on his way to his hotel, he again read the telegram he had received. It was worded as follows :

'Hôtel de ——, Paris, 5.45. You promised to help me if I needed help. Come at once. I am in a position of some danger.—ENA.'

Dudley Massie knew Ena Sherburn well enough to feel sure that she would never have sent him such a telegram had she not earnestly needed someone to assist her. But why send for him ? Why did she not wire to her father ? and what was the nature of the danger she was in ? Morgan Sherburn must be the cause of that danger, or she would have wired to him.

Dudley Massie felt proud of the trust she reposed in him, but he saw at once that if he was not very careful, both Ena and himself might be placed in a compromising position. He cared little for that, personally, provided he could do anything to serve her. He loved Ena Sherburn, but he did not forget she was another man's wife.

A train left Waterloo at 9.45 and caught the midnight boat at Southampton viâ Havre and Rouen. He would reach Paris by noon next day. He hastily put what few things he might require in his portmanteau, and then drove to the station, where he found he had ample time to catch the train.

He had taken his ticket, and was standing on the platform, when he saw one of Morgan Sherburn's grooms, who politely touched his hat to him. In a few moments he was seated in the train, on his way to Southampton and Paris.

As Dudley Massie was being whirled along the railway-line at express speed, the fight at the Fistic Club was taking place.

Shortly before ten o'clock the men stepped

into the ring, and cheer after cheer was given by the vast crowd.

Both men looked fit models for a sculptor, as they stood stripped in the roped ring. Dusky Jim's black skin shone like ebony, and he looked trained to the hour. He sat quietly in his corner, smiling at the crowd, as his trainer and seconds busied themselves in putting the finishing touches to him.

At the opposite corner sat Mick Malone, a perfect Hercules to look at, and with a more confident look upon his face than usual. He had got rid of the idea that Dusky Jim would be the death of him, now he was in the ring. Outside the ring Mick Malone caused his trainer and his backers some anxiety by his faint-heartedness, but once he stepped over the ropes, he seemed to be a different man.

'How do you feel, Mick?' asked his trainer anxiously.

'Fit as a fiddle, Paddy. I'm going to win this fight.'

'That's right, my lad,' said Paddy O'Rorke, for such was the trainer's name. 'Never mind his features—go for his ribs and his heart. These black-fellows can take a heap of head-punching, but when it comes to body blows they flinch.'

Mick Malone nodded, and as he looked round caught sight of his patron, and smiled in a confident manner.

' Looks as though he meant to win,' said Sherburn's companion.

'Yes ; I think he'll win. I never saw him so brimful of confidence before,' said Morgan Sherburn ; and he proceeded to lay odds of five to four in hundreds on Malone with an enthusiastic backer of Dusky Jim.

' Time !' was called, and the men faced each other, and after a hand-shake, smiled defiantly, and the fight commenced.

The first round was more bustling than had been expected, and it was evident Dusky Jim meant to force the pace. Although he pressed his opponent hard, Mick Malone avoided his blows with an agility that was surprising in such a big man. A few seconds before the end of the round Dusky Jim got in a smart blow with his right on Mick Malone's mouth and drew first blood, which caused the admirers of the darkie to shout with joy, and in their momentary enthusiasm to bet even money he won. Whenever he could snap up a wager at evens Morgan Sherburn backed his man, and he smiled as he saw how the black's blow had roused Mick Malone.

Rounds two and three were fought with but little advantage on either side, and it was evident the men were evenly matched.

In round four Mick Malone got in some heavy body blows, which caused Dusky Jim to wince, and at the call of time he went to his corner considerably out of breath. His attendant, however, quickly brought him to, and as he rose for the next round he smiled in such an exasperating manner that Mick Malone went straight for his face. This right-hander was an unlucky blow for Mick, as Dusky Jim got under his guard and gave him a terrific blow on the ribs that brought him to the ground.

As Mick Malone fell with a thud the backers of Dusky Jim became well-nigh frantic with delight.

' I'll lay fifty to forty on the black.'

' Done !' shouted Morgan Sherburn across the room, as he put the wager down in his book.

Mick Malone got on to his feet before he was counted out, and avoided Dusky Jim's blows cleverly.

Up to the tenth round Mick Malone had decidedly the worst of it, but he took his punishment well, and it was evident he was far from beaten.

In the twelfth round Mick showed his best form. He seemed as fresh as when he started, and rained blows heavy and fast upon Dusky Jim's head, neck, and shoulders, but he could not plant a blow on the black's body.

At the end of the round, when Mick Malone went to his corner, Paddy O'Rorke said :

'Why don't you hit his ribs ? It is no good punching his head.'

'I can't,' said Mick. 'His reach is too long, and I can't get under his guard.'

'You'll have to try, if you mean to win,' said Paddy. 'If you keep on at his head he's sure to tire you out.'

The fight was becoming more and more exciting. It was evident the men were in the best of form, and equally determined. Morgan Sherburn began to think it was not such a good thing for Mick Malone as he had imagined.

Fred Lostock was sanguine the darkie would win, and even his usually phlegmatic temper was roused at the great battle he was witnessing.

As for Mick Malone and Dusky Jim, they still came up smiling, and fought round after round fiercely and skilfully. At the end of the fifteenth round honours were divided, and neither man could claim any decided advantage.

Mick Malone's face had been severely mauled, but the black man had only one nasty cut above the right eye, from which the blood slowly trickled, and he wiped it out of his eye from time to time with the back of his hand.

'How is it now, Jim?' asked the darkie's trainer.

'A bit winded, but still fresh. It all depends on who gets in a good knock-out blow. A good heart blow will end the fight. I mean to try for it this time.'

Again the men faced each other, but they did not smile. There was a dogged look on their faces, for each man knew a single blow well delivered would end the match. They sparred carefully, and at the end of the round not a blow had been struck. Three more tame rounds followed, and then came the twentieth.

Somehow the vast audience felt this twentieth round was to be the last. There was a stillness that was almost painful as the men faced each other again. The loud shouts of those anxious to make wagers had ceased. People hardly drew their breath, so great was the tension. Morgan Sherburn was excited, but calm, and he vowed if Mick Malone won he would never forget it. Fred Lostock was uneasy now that he felt the decisive moment was at hand, and wished all was over, and the matter decided one way or the other.

What a round it was, that twentieth in the match between Malone and Coonan! It was talked about for months afterwards, and men grew excited as they related what had taken place. Dusky Jim had the first advantage. He feinted with his right so cleverly that for an instant Mick Malone was off his guard. In a moment, quick as a flash from a cannon, out shot Dusky Jim's left, and caught Mick Malone a tremendous blow in the ribs. The Irishman staggered back, and Dusky Jim, hitting him fairly between the eyes, felled him like an ox.

A hoarse roar from the crowd proclaimed that all was over. But all was not over. Dusky Jim, in the moment of his triumph, sprang back with a peculiar whoop of victory. This seemed to rouse Mick Malone, and, with wonderful pluck and endurance, considering the blows he had just received, he sprang to his feet. For one moment he seemed dazed, but a terrific yell from the crowd roused him. Before the black could recover from his surprise at Mick Malone's sudden revival, the Irish champion was upon him.

Then the scene baffles description. Mick Malone got inside the long reach of the black man. In vain did Dusky Jim try to make use of his long powerful arms. They seemed rather an encumbrance than otherwise. Almost blind, dizzy, and half stunned, Mick Malone's one thought was to reach Dusky Jim's heart. He did not feel any blows the black managed to plant on him at such close quarters.

At last came his chance. With terrific force, considering the time he had been fighting, he drove his fist just under the black's heart.

Dusky Jim gave a gasp, a groan, then a savage growl of defeat, and fell down insensible. Mick Malone towered above him, firm, but well-nigh as insensible as the black man.

Slowly the seconds went by, and when Mick Malone heard Dusky Jim had been counted out, and he had won the fight, his iron nerves gave way, and he fell in a heap across his plucky and prostrate opponent.

CHAPTER XIII.

AFTER THE BATTLE.

THE two champions lay insensible in the ring, and they were the only quiet persons in the great assembly. When Mick Malone reeled and fell, Paddy O'Rorke, followed by the seconds, rushed forward to his assistance, and almost at the same moment Dusky Jim's trainer and his seconds also came to assist their man.

Mick Malone quickly came round, and was led out of the ring amidst a perfect hurricane of cheers, leaning on the shoulder of Paddy O'Rorke. Dusky Jim was carried out still insensible, and a doctor went round to attend to him. Undoubtedly, it had been one of the greatest fights of modern times, and, although defeated, Dusky Jim was by no means disgraced. Opinions were divided as to the actual merits of the contest. The admirers of the black-fellow asserted that Mick Malone's blow was a matter of luck, and had happened by mere chance to hit a vital part. Mick Malone's followers would have none of this, and, whilst admitting that their man was nearly done, vowed he had fought for the blow he

9

aimed, and had schemed admirably to deliver it.

The noise in the club was deafening, and many men became so excited that it required the most strenuous efforts on the part of their friends to prevent their coming to blows.

Morgan Sherburn followed Mick Malone into his dressing-room, and congratulated him on his victory.

'You fought splendidly,' he said. 'I promised to give you a handsome sum if you won, and you shall have it. By Jove! I never saw a more splendid battle, and the black-fellow fought well.'

'You may take your oath about that,' said Mick; 'I never had such a tough job in my life. I hope he's not much hurt. Send and inquire, Paddy. It was a nasty blow I gave him, but I had to put it in to win.'

A messenger was despatched to Dusky Jim's room, and quickly returned with the welcome news that the darkie had come round, and was fairly well again.

'I'll go and shake hands with him,' said Mick.

'You stay here,' said Morgan Sherburn. 'When he comes round, you can both step into the ring and shake hands.'

The people were becoming impatient. Now the fight was over, they were anxious to know how the men fared, and also to gain another sight of them.

They had not long to wait. Mick Malone dressed himself in his ordinary clothes, and stepped over the ropes. It was a proud moment for him as he glanced round at the crowded hall. Handkerchiefs were waved and also hats, and lusty cheers made the place ring again and again.

'I'm glad I won, if only for this,' thought Mick. 'I wonder where Jim is. He deserves cheering as much as I do.'

In a few minutes Dusky Jim appeared, and was also greeted with a storm of cheers. Pearce Holden was much more popular than Morgan Sherburn, and the bulk of those present would have preferred seeing his man win.

Mick Malone stepped forward and grasped Dusky Jim by the hand, and the two men looked very little the worse for their fierce battle.

'You've beaten me fair and square,' said Jim, 'but it was a narrow shave. I don't think there was much between us at the finish.'

'No man ever gave me a better fight,' said

Mick.   Then he added cautiously : ' but I had a good deal left in me at the finish.'

Dusky Jim smiled.   He knew better, and he also knew that if Mick Malone had not got in that heart blow, the fight would in all probability have gone the other way.

' You'll give me my revenge ?' said Jim.

' You'll have to ask the governor about that ; I'm willing,' said Mick.

Pearce Holden was not satisfied with the result of the fight, and asked Morgan Sherburn for a return battle.   Elated with the victory of his man, Morgan Sherburn said that, provided Mick Malone was willing, he would back him to fight Dusky Jim again in six months' time for a similar stake.

The men were consulted, and before they left the ring it was publicly announced another match had been arranged between them.   This gave great satisfaction, and the backers of Dusky Jim were sanguine they would get their money back.

Fred Lostock took the defeat of the man he had backed quite philosophically, and meant to back him again when he had the chance.

' I'm sorry, for Massie's sake, he lost,' said Fred to himself.   ' I wonder if he will find it inconvenient to pay. If so, he must let me help him out.'

He met Morgan Sherburn as he was leaving the club, and said to him :

'You have won a heavy stake, I hear. It was a splendid fight. I shall back the darkie again next time.'

'And lose your money again,' said Morgan Sherburn. 'You need not run away with the idea that knock-out blow of Malone's was a fluke, for he was fighting for it all the time.'

'The very reason I think it a pure accident he got it in at the finish. He was dead-beat at the time and hitting wildly, and I do not think he knew where he was striking,' said Fred.

'You fellows are never satisfied when you are beaten,' said Sherburn. 'Holden is of the same opinion as yourself, and that is why he has made another match. He is sure to lose his money again. Was Dudley Massie present ? I thought I saw him leave shortly before the fight commenced.'

'He had a wire from home,' said Fred. 'Important business. He was awfully sorry to miss the fight.'

'It must have been something urgent to make him leave in such a hurry,' said Sherburn.

'He didn't even see the good fight Jim gave him for his money.'

When Morgan Sherburn came down to breakfast next morning, his valet was home again from Paris.

'Everything passed off well?' said Morgan Sherburn to him.

'Yes, sir; I had no trouble whatever.'

'You will be glad to hear Mick Malone won the fight. It was a tight fit, but he got in a telling blow at the finish. I owe you a hundred, and I will give you a cheque for it when you wish.'

'I'm rather pressed for money,' said Daly. 'I should like the cheque as soon as convenient.'

Morgan Sherburn smiled as he said

'You are always short of money I really don't know what you do with it. You have no occasion to spend much, situated as you are here.'

'Pardon me, sir,' said Raymond Daly, 'but that is just where you make a mistake. When a valet has a wealthy master, it behoves him to keep up appearances by spending money freely. I spend more than you imagine, and in your interest.'

'Oh!' said Morgan Sherburn, 'then I expect, with so many drains upon your purse, on my behalf, you will be asking for an advance in your wages.'

'That was what I thought of doing,' said Daly. 'I think my services are worth more.'

'And supposing I think you are very well paid, overpaid, in fact, and decline to grant your request ?'

Raymond Daly smiled and replied :

'You are such a generous master that I do not think you will refuse my modest request.'

'I'll think the matter over,' said Morgan Sherburn ; 'but, remember, you have made several calls upon me.'

'True, sir,' said Daly ; 'but this last service may be as dangerous as it is important.'

'I thought you told me you did not understand the meaning of the wire you sent?' said Sherburn.

'I have studied it carefully,' said Daly. 'I had ample time to do so, and I think I have a clue to its meaning.'

'Very good indeed,' remarked Morgan Sherburn ; 'and if you have a clue, I presume it is your intention to follow it up.'

'I never betray secrets.'

'When it is made worth your while to keep them,' said Sherburn.

Raymond Daly bowed, as much as to say :

' Put it which way you like : it does not matter to me, if I handle your money.'

' You have been an excellent servant,' said Morgan Sherburn. 'When your proposal for an increase of salary is made, I do not think it will be refused.'

' You are always just,' said Daly, as he left the room.

' You shall have plenty of justice, my man, once I catch you tripping,' thought Morgan Sherburn, as he watched the door close behind his valet.

Morgan Sherburn was on good terms with himself the day after the fight, and he determined to leave for Paris, in order to ascertain how his plot had worked.

He was walking down Piccadilly, when he came across Sir Gordon Sefton. They were mutually surprised to see each other

' I thought you were still in Paris,' said Sir Gordon. ' When did you return home ? Rather unexpected, is it not ? I hope there is nothing wrong.'

' I never expected to meet you,' said Morgan Sherburn. ' The truth of the matter is, I had a most important engagement in town. It was made before my marriage, and I forgot all about it until I received a letter in Paris. I explained the whole matter to Ena, and asked her to accompany me to London, but she preferred to remain in Paris, and I am going back as quickly as possible.'

'Ena alone in Paris!' exclaimed Sir Gordon. 'You have not been married very long. I cannot understand it.'

'She has her maid,' said Morgan Sherburn, 'and it is entirely her own choice that she remained behind. She was mighty independent about it, and said she should do exactly as she liked. I am afraid I shall have some difficulty in managing her. She is inclined to kick over the traces already. It is a false start, and she will have to be pulled up.'

Sir Gordon Sefton did not like Morgan Sherburn's tone, but he thought it better not to interfere at present. He knew Ena was far better able to take care of herself than most women.

'It must have been very urgent business to separate you from your wife during the honeymoon,' said Sir Gordon.

'It was; and I may add that I am a considerable gainer by keeping my appointment. Yesterday meant a gain of several thousands to me.'

'I am glad to hear it,' said Sir Gordon.

'Fortune generally showers her favours on you very rich men.'

'You have no cause to complain of fortune's favours,' said Morgan Sherburn.

'No; I cannot say I have,' replied Sir Gordon.   'When do you return to Paris?'

'Probably to-night, or by the morning express,' said Morgan Sherburn.

'I return to Sefton to-day,' said Sir Gordon. 'Perhaps it will be better if I do not mention I have seen you to Lady Sefton.   She would think it strange Ena should be in Paris alone.'

'As you think best,' said Sherburn.

They parted, and Sherburn went to his club. He remained there some time, and was driving in a hansom to Park Lane when he met Marie de Tourville on her way to the theatre in her brougham.   She hailed him, and he stopped his cab, paid the driver, and stepped into the brougham.

Miss de Tourville's language to him was more forcible than polite.   She had not met him since his marriage, and she upbraided him for his perfidy in vigorous terms.

'I never promised to marry you, Marie,' he said.   'You have no cause to grumble.'

'But I have—there, I hate her!   I've never seen her; but I hear she's beautiful, and an awful swell; been presented at Court, and all that. My! what ever could she see in you to jump at? I guess your shekels attracted her. Well, I don't wonder at it, for you're powerful rich, and can buy anything you want.'

Morgan Sherburn did not relish this speech, but he had no desire to quarrel with Marie de Tourville.

'We will leave my wife out of the question,' he said. 'She is in Paris, and I mean to have a jolly time.'

'But you have only been married a few days!' she exclaimed.

'What of that,' he said. 'Married people do as they like nowadays.'

'Not knowing, can't say,' replied his companion; 'but here we are at the theatre. Are you coming behind?'

'No, thanks; I'll see you later on,' he said.

She waved her hand, and vanished at the stage entrance.

CHAPTER XIV

A SURPRISE FOR SHERBURN.

WHEN Dudley Massie arrived in Paris, and was loitering about the station in a hesitating way, it occurred to him he might have been duped, and sent on a fool's errand. During the journey some such thoughts had passed through his mind, but he had put them aside. Now he was in Paris, and near Ena Sherburn, these doubts arose again with redoubled force. Was the telegram genuine? If so, it was clearly his duty to respond to her call for aid, because he had promised to do so. If not genuine, then, who had sent it?

After some time spent in reflection, he came to the conclusion the wire was genuine ; because he could think of no one who had a reason for sending it except Ena Sherburn. It seemed absurd to him to imagine, as he had done for a few moments, that Morgan Sherburn had sent it, because there was no reason why he should do so. Dudley Massie was not the man to suspect such underhand proceedings as Morgan Sherburn was capable of.

'Hang it all!' he said to himself, 'I am in

Paris in response to this telegram, and the best thing for me to do is to see Ena Sherburn as soon as possible.'

Having decided upon this course, Dudley walked to the hotel named in the telegram, and inquired for Mrs. Sherburn, sending in his card.

When the card was presented to Ena Sherburn, she gave a slight exclamation of surprise. The name of Dudley Massie was the last she expected to see presented to her, and she could not understand why he was in Paris, and why he had called upon her.

There would be no harm in seeing him, she thought, and was angry with herself because she knew it would give her pleasure to see him. Now she was married, and a barrier placed between herself and Dudley Massie, she was far more inclined to make a friend of him than when she was merely Miss Sefton. She felt that with Dudley Massie she was safe, or, rather, her reputation was safe.

Ena Sherburn was not a woman to give way to mere feelings of passion and designate them love. She had never loved any man so far in her life, nor had she even verged upon it. She was not devoid of the feelings that inspire love, but they had never been roused in her.

She twisted the card in her fingers for a few moments, and then signified that she would see Mr. Massie.

When Dudley Massie entered the room, and looked at Ena Sherburn, he knew there was a mistake somewhere. The woman he had come to help evidently stood in no need of assistance. She gave him a cordial greeting that at once dispelled any lingering doubts he might have had upon the subject.

'This is an unexpected pleasure, Mr. Massie,' she said. 'What brings you to Paris?'

He hesitated to reply. He was thinking whether it would be best to tell her why he had come, or merely to lead her to think he was in Paris on business. He quickly decided that, as the telegram had been sent in her name, she ought to know of it.

'This brought me to Paris,' he said, handing her the telegram, and watching her face as she read it.

Ena Sherburn took the telegram, and read it. She was so astonished that she repeated it aloud:

'You promised to help me if I needed help. Come at once. I am in a position of some danger.'

'It is sent in my name,' she said. 'What is the meaning of it?'

'You did not send it?' he asked. 'I merely ask you as a matter of form, because I see you did not. When I received it, I naturally responded to it, and came at once. You may remember I promised to help you if ever you needed a friend, and you did me the honour to say you would accept such help. It was my duty to come and see you, and I am here. My next duty will be to find out who sent this telegram, and then with what object it was sent.'

Ena Sherburn saw at once that Dudley Massie spoke the truth. She knew he had no hand in sending such a telegram merely to have an excuse to call upon her during her husband's absence. Did he know her husband was absent from Paris? She would ask him.

'Are you aware Mr. Sherburn is in London?' she asked.

'Yes,' replied Dudley Massie; 'I saw him before I left London.'

'Then, why do you come to me, knowing I am alone?' she said angrily, and growing unreasonable in her anger.

'The only excuse I have to offer you know already,' he said. 'It is not necessary for me to remain longer, but I give you my assurance I will find out who sent that telegram.'

He rose to go, but Ena Sherburn did not wish him to leave her.

'Sit down, Mr. Massie,' she said. 'I am not blaming you for what has happened, but I might be placed in a compromising position through this telegram.' Then, realizing what she had said, she blushed slightly, and added hastily 'That is hardly what I mean. Of course, there has been some mistake.'

'I do not think so,' said Dudley. 'The telegram was sent for some purpose. Have you any enemy who wishes you ill, and would do you an injury, if possible?'

'I can think of no one,' she replied. And then, remembering how Morgan Sherburn had left her, and what she had discovered of his character, she added: 'Where did you see Mr. Sherburn?'

'At the Fistic Club,' said Dudley.

'What was he there for? Does he often visit there?'

'Oh yes, frequently,' said Massie. 'He backed Malone to beat Coonan, and the fight came off last night.'

'So this was the "important business" that called him home,' she thought. 'He left me

alone in Paris during our honeymoon to attend
a prize-fight.'

She almost hated him at the mere thought
of how he had degraded her by marrying her,
and yet she accepted his offer with her eyes
fully opened to his serious defects.

' Did you go there to see the fight ?' she asked.

' I did,' replied Massie.

' I am sorry,' she said softly. ' It is a
degrading exhibition.'

The tone in which she spoke made his heart
beat fast. He was very much in love with
Ena Sherburn.

' If it will give you pleasure, I will never
attend another fight,' he said quickly

' Give *me* pleasure !' she said coldly. ' What
can it possibly have to do with me whether
you attend such places or otherwise ? It is no
concern of mine.'

And yet she was pleased he answered her as
he did.

He made no reply, but took the rebuke in
silence, and considered it well merited.

' Did my husband know when you left the
club ?'

' He saw me go out, no doubt,' said Massie.
' It was shortly before the fight commenced.'

' Were the stakes heavy ?'

10

'A thousand a side.'

'And you do not know who won?'

'No.'

'Are you interested in the result?'

'Yes,' he replied, wondering why she questioned him.

'Pardon my inquisitiveness if I ask you if you had any wager with Mr. Sherburn over this fight,' she said.

'I had a bet of five hundred pounds with him on Coonan against Malone.'

'That is a large sum for you to bet, Mr. Massie.'

'It is. I shall never wager that amount again. I was chaffed into it, and ought to have known better.'

'By Mr. Sherburn?' she asked.

'Yes; if you must know,' he said. 'But why ask all these questions?'

'Mr. Sherburn dislikes you?' she asked.

'We are not good friends,' said Dudley.

'Perhaps you are not aware he left me alone in Paris during our honeymoon in order to attend this fight?' she said sarcastically.

'The brute!' thought Massie. Aloud he said: 'Probably he had made the match some time before you were married, and then forgotten about it until he was reminded of it.'

'Pray do not make excuses for him. He is no friend of yours or mine,' she said.

Dudley Massie thought Ena had soon found out she had made a mistake in marrying Morgan Sherburn, but she knew what to expect when she married him.

'He certainly is no friend of mine,' said Massie; 'but I should be sorry to think he was not a friend of yours.'

'You must return to London at once,' said Ena, 'before your absence is noticed. The sender of this telegram evidently wishes our names to be connected in some way. Scandal is the great weapon of small-minded individuals. They find they can do much hurt at very little risk to themselves. When you reach London, will you kindly take a letter from me and deliver it to Mr. Sherburn? When he has read it, hand him the telegram you received.'

'I have no desire to call upon Mr. Sherburn,' said Dudley Massie, 'but I will do so if you wish it.'

'I do wish it. It is of the utmost importance you should deliver my letter, and produce the telegram yourself. Remember, racing men are very suspicious,' she added, with a smile. 'Excuse me while I write the letter.'

She opened a door and passed into another room.

Dudley Massie wondered what would come of it all. He was not quick at grasping such a situation as this, although he had all his wits about him in a tight place in a race. He felt glad Ena trusted him, and was proud of her confidence.

'What a beautiful, stately woman she is!' he thought. 'The mere idea of her being married to a little beast like Sherburn makes me wild. I'd like to punch his head. Hang me if I don't if I get the chance!'

Ena Sherburn returned and handed him a letter addressed to her husband.

'Give him this,' she said, 'and then show him the telegram.'

'I will go there as soon as I arrive in town,' he said. 'Good-bye.'

He held out his hand, and she put hers in it, and the mere contact thrilled him.

'I am very much obliged to you for coming,' she said. 'It proves to me, if proof were needed, that I can always rely upon you to help me.'

She allowed him to retain her hand while she spoke, and then gently withdrew it.

When the door closed behind him, Ena

Sherburn sat down on the sofa, and said to herself :

' *He* is a man, at any rate. What to call Morgan Sherburn I hardly know. I feel confident he sent that telegram, or caused it to be sent. He wishes to compromise me in order that he may have more power over me. We shall see, Morgan Sherburn. We have only been married a few days, and you have already made two serious mistakes. The first was to prefer a prize-fight to your wife's society, and the second was to clumsily try and damage her good name to suit your own ends. You shall suffer for this, and perhaps Mr. Massie will help me. He will if I ask him, but I must be merciful and spare him.' She smiled as she thought what power a woman of her beauty and brains holds over men who appreciate both.

When Dudley Massie arrived in London next morning, he called at Sherburn's house in Park Lane shortly before noon, and found that worthy at breakfast.

Judging from his appearance, Morgan Sherburn had been having a night out. He looked dissipated and untidy. His eyes were bloodshot, and his hands shook. He was pulling himself together by frequent applications of brandy-and-soda. He was in an irritable frame of mind, and scowled at his unexpected visitor.

' To what do I owe this honour?' he sneered. ' Have you come to pay your wager? Sorry you missed the fight, for I never saw a better. You'll have a chance of getting your revenge, for the men fight again in six months. You can keep the cash and go double or quits if you like, for I don't suppose you are too flush of the ready.'

' I have come to deliver this letter to you,' said Dudley Massie. ' As to the wager, that will be paid at once, and I decline to bet with you again.'

' Oh, indeed!' sneered Morgan Sherburn, ' are you afraid you'll not be paid if you win?'

' No. You do not as a rule make bad debts, although it may come to that some day.'

Morgan Sherburn did not reply. He was too much surprised at seeing his wife's handwriting on the envelope that had been handed to him.

' Why, this is from my wife!' he gasped. ' How the deuce did you get hold of it?'

' Read the letter, and no doubt you will find out,' said Dudley Massie.

CHAPTER XV.

WHAT FOLLOWED THE SURPRISE.

MORGAN SHERBURN read his wife's letter slowly, and the contents surprised him. He fancied he had been very clever, and the discovery that his wife had seen through his clumsy, despicable action did not improve his temper.

Ena Sherburn knew how to write a cutting letter. Her sarcasm was not lost upon her husband, and he winced under the sting of her words. Dudley Massie saw him wince, and this was an additional annoyance to him. He began to read the letter a second time, in order to consider how he should act. He wondered if Dudley Massie knew the contents of the letter, and then he thought Ena had more respect for herself than to make a confidant of any man. He looked up at Dudley Massie, when he had read the letter a second time, as though he expected him to speak.

' I was to hand you this telegram when you had read the letter,' said Massie.

'You appear to have received very precise instructions from my wife,' said Morgan Sherburn. He knew the contents of the telegram, but he read it in order to try to deceive Massie.

'Upon my word,' he said, 'this is a cool business! My wife sends you a telegram to meet her in Paris when I am in London, and then she coolly makes you the bearer of an impertinent letter to me, and asks you to produce her telegram as corroborative evidence of her disgraceful conduct. So this was the reason of your sudden departure from the club,' he added, holding up the telegram. 'My wife's attractions must be very uncommon to tempt you away from such a splendid fight.'

'It is a pity you do not appreciate your wife's attractions a little more,' said Dudley Massie. 'It is not very complimentary to her to prefer a prize-fight to her society.'

'That's my business,' said Morgan Sherburn. 'As for this telegram, I shall want to know the meaning of it, and why it was sent.'

'That is precisely what I want to know,' said Dudley Massie. 'Your wife did not send me that telegram, and no one knows that better than yourself. Probably you also know who did send it. If so, I shall be glad if you will give me his name. I do not choose to be made a dupe of, nor to have my name connected with your wife.'

' Do you mean to insinuate I had a hand in sending this telegram ?' asked Sherburn.

' Yes,' said Dudley Massie, ' or you would not have put such a question to me.'

' Take care what you say, or I will make it uncomfortable for you,' said Sherburn.

' I am not afraid of anything you can do,' said Dudley Massie with contempt.

' But you may be afraid of what I can do to my wife, with such a telegram as this in my possession,' said Sherburn.

' You dare not attempt to cast any slur upon your wife's name,' said Dudley Massie ; ' even you would not be such a blackguard as that.'

' Actions for divorce have been founded upon less evidence,' said Morgan Sherburn. ' I have made a bad bargain, and am not at all sure I shall not try and get out of it. I made up my mind to marry Ena Sefton, and, having done so, I am satisfied ; but I did not bargain for her encouraging any old lovers she might have had before I met her.'

Dudley Massie felt he should not be able to control himself if this conversation was carried much further. He wondered how Ena Sefton ever condescended to marry such a man.

' You have no occasion to talk about actions

for divorce,' said Dudley Massie ; 'your conduct is too well known for that. You disgrace your wife by your vileness. Some day you will be thrashed by a man who respects your wife and despises you.'

'Meaning yourself,' sneered Morgan. 'You may be a bigger man than I am, but I doubt if you could carry out your amiable intention of thrashing me.'

Dudley Massie smiled. He felt at the moment he could have kicked Sherburn downstairs, and given him a thrashing into the bargain.

The smile exasperated Morgan Sherburn, and he said angrily :

'You will smile on the other side of your face before long if you try and worm yourself into my wife's good graces behind my back.'

'Take care,' said Dudley Massie. 'Dare to say one word against your wife, and I shall not be able to keep my hands off you.'

'A brawl in my house about the fair fame of my wife would no doubt please her immensely,' said Morgan Sherburn. 'Perhaps you would relish it. It would be a cheap way of getting your names coupled.'

Dudley Massie stepped towards the speaker

in a threatening attitude, but Sherburn did not flinch. He poured out more brandy, and then uncorked a large soda.

'You must be drunk,' said Massie ; 'that is the only poor excuse I can offer for your conduct. Give me the telegram back. I have done as your wife requested, and now I have heard what you have said, I am convinced you had a hand in sending it. Why you did so is best known to yourself. It was a contemptible action, but not unworthy of you.'

'I shall keep this telegram,' said Morgan Sherburn ; 'it may come in useful some day.'

'Hand it over to me,' said Dudley Massie. 'It is not your property It was given to me by your wife, and it was delivered to me from Paris. You have no right to detain it.'

'I have every right now it has come into my possession,' said Sherburn. 'It is my duty to take care to preserve such a valuable document.'

'Are you going to hand it to me?' asked Massie firmly.

'No,' said Sherburn.

'Then I shall take it from you,' replied Massie.

Morgan Sherburn pushed back his chair and stepped towards the door. Before Dudley

Massie could stop him he had blown a whistle, and in response to it two powerful rough-looking fellows appeared on the scene. Dudley Massie saw at a glance they were a couple of the lower class of fighting-men that Morgan Sherburn often had hanging round him and sponging on him.

'You can try and take the telegram from me now if you wish,' said Sherburn.

Dudley Massie saw it would be useless to attempt such a thing, and was sorry he had allowed the telegram to go out of his possession. It was his property, and he could legally claim it, but that would give publicity to an affair that had much better remain unknown.

'When a man surrounds himself with hired ruffians,' said Dudley Massie, 'honest men have no chance of fair-play Take care that such men do not turn upon you. You are welcome to keep the telegram you caused to be sent to me until such time as I legally claim it.'

When Dudley Massie called these men 'hired ruffians,' they looked fierce, and he would probably have fared badly for his rash words had not Morgan Sherburn interfered.

'I want no row here,' said Sherburn. 'You will know Mr. Massie again, and you can settle your score with him in your own way.'

' I am not afraid,' said Dudley Massie ; ' I
shall find means to defend myself.'

He went downstairs, opened the door himself,
and passed out of the house.

He walked down Park Lane and crossed
over into Hyde Park, which was well-nigh
deserted. A brisk walk made him feel on
better terms with himself. He made up his
mind to go back to Five Oaks Farm at once.
He was sick of the whole business, and hated
Morgan Sherburn for his paltry conduct. He
knew what capital a man like Sherburn could
make out of such a telegram, even if he had
been instrumental in sending it.

When he reached Five Oaks, however, he
quickly shook off any feeling of depression he
felt, and at once went to work at the Sefton
stables. Nothing suited Dudley Massie better
than the management of a few good horses,
and in Sir Gordon Sefton he had an employer
in a thousand.

Sir Gordon was not a suspicious man, and
never came prying about the stables extracting
information from the men under his manager.
He liked Dudley Massie and had confidence
in him, although he rather doubted his judgment in regard to The Slogger.

A day or two after Dudley Massie returned

to Sefton, Sir Gordon came to the stables to look round.   He knew Dudley Massie had gone to London to see the fight at the Fistic Club, and he also knew his son-in-law had backed the winner.

One of his first questions was :

' Well, Massie, how did you like the fight ? What do you think of it ?   Some people hold the opinion that it was a fluke, and that the darkie was unlucky to be knocked out.'

' I did not see the fight,' replied Dudley Massie in a hesitating manner most unusual to him.   ' I went to the Fistic Club, but a telegram I received necessitated my leaving before the fight.   I was awfully sorry to miss it, but it could not be helped.'

' It must have been something important to cause you to miss the fight,' said Sir Gordon.

' It was,' replied Dudley Massie ; ' and I was very much annoyed about it.'

' I am sorry you were not there,' replied Sir Gordon.   ' You could have told me all about it, and I have heard you give a graphic description of a fight before.   Mr. Sherburn was there, I believe ?'

' Yes,' replied Massie ; ' and he must have had a good win.'

' I wonder if he knows Sherburn left his wife

in Paris,' thought Sir Gordon. 'Probably not, but it is sure to get about, and people will think it strange they should be separated during their wedding tour. It is awkward— very awkward! I wish Sherburn had more tact and consideration. Hang it all! I wish Ena had not chosen him. A fine girl, too. Well, there's no accounting for tastes.'

Sir Gordon quickly banished these somewhat unpleasant thoughts, and said :

'When shall we run The Slogger? He ought to have a trial in public before the National.'

'I think Derby would be the best place,' said Dudley ; 'there are one or two good races there he might be entered in. We know the sort of weight he will get, and he would stand a chance.'

'I have been looking over the list,' said Sir Gordon. 'There's the Shipley Hall Handi- cap Steeplechase Plate of ninety sovereigns— about three miles ; that ought to suit him. There will be no penalty if he wins, and some good horses generally run in it.'

'The race I should pick for him myself,' replied Dudley Massie. 'He will get about seven pounds more than he has in the Grand National, which will bring him up to ten stone seven pounds, or thereabouts, according to the handicap, and I can ride him easily enough at that weight, but I must get a bit off for the big race at Liverpool.'

' Is there anything else we can enter ?' asked Sir Gordon.

' There's Off Chance ; he's four, and can be entered for the Juvenile Steeplechase Plate, two miles,' said Dudley.

' Is he forward enough ?' asked Sir Gordon. ' I fancied you were going to keep him for another season.'

' He is a much better horse than I fancied he was,' said Dudley. ' He is in the Grand National with nine stone seven pounds. I don't think he has a chance in that race, of course, but he might win the Juvenile Plate.'

' It will do him no harm to give him a run,' said Sir Gordon, ' provided his condition is good enough.'

' He is all right in that respect,' said Dudley.

' You can ride him, of course ?' said Sir Gordon.

' Yes,' replied Dudley ; ' the weight is ten stone ten pounds each, so I shall have to put up a bit of dead weight, but not much—a few pounds.'

' I shall go to Derby to see them run,' said

Sir Gordon. 'I wonder if Sherburn will enter anything.'

'Sure to do,' said Dudley. 'He never misses the chance of a ride, and the season will soon be over.'

'Then, we shall perhaps get a line as to the chance of Snowstorm for the National.'

'Mr. Sherburn likes to keep people in the dark,' said Dudley. 'We may get some idea of how Snowstorm will shape, although I doubt it ; and if he runs in the Shipley Hall Plate, I shall try and take his measure.'

CHAPTER XVI.

A GOOD JUVENILE.

SIR GORDON SEFTON'S horses were duly entered at Derby, and when the handicap came out for the Shipley Hall Plate, The Slogger stood on the ten stone twelve mark—a few pounds more than Dudley Massie had fancied he would receive.

Morgan Sherburn had three horses entered, Snowstorm and Old Tor in the same race as The Slogger, and Mitre in the Juvenile Plate. Snowstorm had received a few pounds more than The Slogger, and Sherburn grumbled accordingly.

When Sir Gordon and Dudley Massie decided to run the horses, The Slogger and Off Chance were given some strong work, and they both did so well on it that their trainer thought they had a good chance of pulling off both events. Sir Gordon watched them at their work, and gave Dudley Massie credit for training them so well.

Dudley was often at Sefton House, where he spent most of his time in amusing Arthur Sefton. The unfortunate lad seemed to lean upon Dudley Massie, and regard him as an elder brother. When Arthur Sefton felt equal to it, Dudley Massie would have him taken to the stables in his invalid chair, and the lad's eyes brightened and his cheeks had a healthier glow as he watched the horses he would have loved to ride.

The Slogger was now Arthur's pet fancy, and he watched the horse's gradual improvement in condition with keen eyes. Arthur Sefton was a good judge of a horse, and he knew The Slogger had 'come on' wonderfully since he had been in the Sefton stables.

'How Morgan Sherburn must regret he ever parted with The Slogger!' said Arthur one morning, when he had been wheeled down to the stables by Dudley Massie.

'He'll regret it more than ever when he sees The Slogger run at Derby,' said Dudley.

'Do you think he will win there?' asked Arthur eagerly.

'I am very confident about it,' replied Dudley; 'and as I ride him myself, I shall know exactly how to handle him. It is a pretty good thing; but why are you so anxious about it?'

'Because I dislike Morgan Sherburn,' said Arthur sharply. 'If I were a man, and had my health and strength, I would let him know what I thought about his conduct to my sister. Ena is not my favourite, but she is my sister, and therefore it makes me wild to hear of her being insulted.'

Dudley Massie was surprised to hear Arthur speak in this tone, and wondered if he could have heard about the forged telegram. On second thought, he knew this was not likely.

'What has Morgan Sherburn been doing now?' asked Dudley.

'He left my sister alone in Paris, in order to attend a beastly prize-fight. I heard the governor tell my mother,' said Arthur.

'That was hardly the sort of conduct to

expect from a newly - married man,' said Dudley.

'Were you very fond of Ena?' asked Arthur suddenly.

Dudley Massie was rather taken aback at the question, but he laughed and said :

'I admired your sister very much, but, of course, in a respectful way She was not likely to regard a man in my position with much favour.'

'It would have been a thousand times better for her if she had married you,' said Arthur. 'As for respectability, your family is as good as ours—if not better. I wish you liked Beatrice. She is worth a dozen Enas.'

Dudley Massie laughed again, as he said :

'I am afraid you are a bit of a Radical. I do like your sister Beatrice very much ; who could help doing so, when she is so kind to you?'

'You're a good fellow,' said Arthur, 'and therefore I'll let you into a secret. Beatrice is very much in love with you. Oh, don't pretend it is all rubbish ! I have quick eyes, and I know Beaty better than she knows herself. Take my advice, and forget Ena, because it will only get you into trouble to think of her. Beatrice is the girl for you. I have set my

heart upon it, so please do not offer any objections.'

'You are a regular matchmaker,' said Dudley,
who could not help being amused at the evident
earnestness of Arthur's manner.

'Matchmaker? Not I!' exclaimed Arthur.
'I've seen quite enough of matchmaking. Ena
and Morgan Sherburn are fine examples of the
beauty and holiness of marriages not made in
heaven.'

'Cynic!' said Dudley.

'A cynic is a snarler,' replied Arthur. 'You
are complimentary. I am not a cynic, because
I don't snarl. To change the subject, which I
will renew again at a more favourable time,
will you oblige me by putting a tenner on The
Slogger for me in the Shipley Hall Plate?'

'What wild extravagance is this?' said
Dudley, who loved to chaff Arthur, and make
him cheerful and spirited. 'A sovereign is
more in your line. Rash youth! I must tell
your father of your fast-growing gambling
propensities.'

'Tell my father if I lose,' said Arthur—'or,
rather, I will do it myself. He will then know
what an impoverished condition I am in, and
will replenish my exchequer.'

'What a blessing it is to have a father to

draw upon in case of emergency,' replied Dudley.

'Stop chaffing, or I shall leave you,' said Arthur. 'Seriously, will you put me a ten-pound note on The Slogger? I can spare that easily out of my allowance. The dear old governor is very good to me,' he added wistfully.

'Take my advice, and have five pounds on Off Chance in the Juvenile Plate, and if he wins, put the lot on The Slogger,' said Dudley.

'Bother Off Chance!' said Arthur. 'I don't like the horse or his name. Let me have a look at him.'

Dudley Massie wheeled Arthur to Off Chance's box, and the lad looked the horse over with critical eyes.

'There's a vast improvement in him since the last time I saw him,' said Arthur. 'You do put a polish on them. I'll take your advice. You can put me a fiver on this fellow, and play it up on The Slogger if it comes off.'

Such jaunts as these round the stables Arthur Sefton eagerly looked forward to, and always returned to the house in a much better temper.

The Derby Hunt Meeting was generally well attended, because several candidates for Liverpool honours were given a run here. The

first day of the meeting passed off successfully,
and Off Chance and The Slogger arrived in
ample time for their races on the second day.

One of the first men Dudley Massie met in the
paddock was Morgan Sherburn, who scowled at
him in his usual manner. It was seldom Morgan
Sherburn was seen at a race-meeting without
a scowl on his face. He had a keen, cunning
look about him, and tried to give men an idea
that he was very clever at the great game. It
was, however, a well-known fact that he had
been 'had' on many occasions by men he
considered far below his standard of turf
tactics.

'Sherburn looks gloomier than ever,' said
Fred Lostock, who had run down to Derby
to see how Sir Gordon's horses shaped.

'He'll be positively black in the face after
the Shipley Hall Steeplechase,' said Dudley.

'Are you going to win with The Slogger?'

'If I can ; and I think he has a chance,' said
Dudley.

'There are one or two good horses in,' said
Fred. 'There's Bohemia, Jumbo, St. Elmo,
Snowstorm, and one or two more. If you beat
them, The Slogger will be more fancied than
he is now for the National. Has this juvenile of
yours any chance ?'

' A very fair one,' said Dudley.

' Then I shall have a bit on,' said Fred Lostock.

There were ten runners for the Juvenile Steeplechase Plate, and Morgan Sherburn backed Mitre heavily, and the horse quickly became a hot favourite. Several horses were backed, but Off Chance was not much fancied, and stood at eight to one.

' Have you backed him?' asked Fred Lostock.

' I have put a " pony " on him,' replied Sir Gordon ; ' that is quite as much as I care to risk. Massie fancies him more than I do.'

' Massie's a good judge,' thought Fred, and proceeded to invest a modest amount on Off Chance.

Morgan Sherburn rode Mitre, and was confident of winning. He had tried Mitre with Snowstorm, and the former had acquitted himself creditably.

At the post Dudley Massie kept Off Chance away from Mitre, on whom Sherburn seemed slightly uncomfortable.

The lot got away level, and Dudley Massie kept Off Chance well in hand. He knew two miles over these jumps would steady the majority of runners carrying ten stone ten pounds each.

Chat made the running, and when half the distance had been safely got over Mitre went on in front.

Dudley Massie saw it was time to set Off Chance going, as he did not wish Mitre to steal a march on him.

At the last fence Mitre led, but he blundered, and although Sherburn got him safely over, he lost several lengths. Off Chance cleared the obstacle in fine style, and a great race ensued down the straight.

The favourite held his own, and looked like winning with a bit in hand.

Dudley Massie had, however, been nursing his mount, and Off Chance came with such a brilliant run that he quickly drew level with Mitre. When Morgan Sherburn saw Off Chance draw level with him he began to ride Mitre savagely, and the horse swerved under the punishment, and slightly interfered with Off Chance. Sherburn had made too much use of the favourite early in the race, and although Mitre struggled gamely on, he was beaten by a clear length by Off Chance.

The performance of Sir Gordon's horse was regarded as good, for it had become public property that Mitre had been well tried with Sherburn's Grand National candidate.

'That's a very promising juvenile you have,' said one of the stewards to Sir Gordon Sefton. 'He will be a good second string for the Grand National. Rather too bad of you to beat your son-in-law in this way.'

'Mr. Sherburn can afford to take care of himself,' replied Sir Gordon. 'Off Chance is much better than I expected. As you say, Colonel, he will be a valuable second string.'

Sir Gordon walked towards the paddock, and as Colonel —— looked after him, he said to himself :

'There's no love lost between Sefton and his precious son-in-law. Sherburn will have to keep an eye on that dashing wife of his, or she'll hold the whip hand, and then kick over the traces.'

'Beat you this time,' said Sir Gordon to Morgan Sherburn.

'You just scrambled home,' was the reply. 'My horse swerved at the finish, or the result would have been different. Doesn't it strike you as being rather foolish to run our horses against each other? With yours out of the way, Mitre would have walked in, and Off Chance would have been a fine rod in pickle for another day.'

'Massie thought Off Chance would win ; and

as I like to see my colours on winners, I ran him,' said Sir Gordon.

'It is a cutthroat policy, nevertheless,' said Sherburn. 'I'm one of the family now, and you might consider me a little. I lost a lot of money over the race.'

Sir Gordon winced at the expression, 'one of the family.' He was not at all proud of his son-in-law. He replied rather haughtily :

'Because you married my daughter, it is no reason why we should race together. I think it far better to keep our racing matters entirely separate. There will be no chance of any misunderstanding or unpleasantness then.'

'Conceited old fool!' muttered Sherburn to himself as Sir Gordon went on to congratulate Dudley Massie on his win.

Sir Gordon met Massie coming from the telegraph-office, and said to him :

'You rode a fine race, and I am very pleased with the win.'

'I have just sent your son a wire : he will be delighted,' said Dudley. 'I put a trifle on for him.'

Sir Gordon smiled kindly as he said :

'It is very good of you to remember Arthur. I do not know what the lad would do without you.'

'I must weigh out for The Slogger now,' said Dudley. 'He ought to win the Shipley Hall Plate comfortably, for he can give Off Chance a lot of weight, and beat him badly.'

'Try and take the measure of Snowstorm,' said Sir Gordon.

'I will if I have a chance,' said Dudley; 'but the horse goes badly in the betting. I am afraid Mr. Sherburn will not ride him out. He may be merely going for a feeler.'

Sir Gordon Sefton's face clouded. He was a thorough good sportsman, and he hated to hear of horses going badly in the betting. He was the more annoyed because it happened to be Sherburn's horse that was going badly in this instance.

'I'll give Morgan a bit of my mind if I see anything suspicious in his riding,' said Sir Gordon to himself.

CHAPTER XVII.

HOW SNOWSTORM BEAT THE SLOGGER.

FRED LOSTOCK won money over Off Chance, and he wished to further increase his gains by backing the right horse in the next race. He noticed how badly Snowstorm went in the betting, and thought Morgan Sherburn was up to some of his little tricks.

'I never can tell what Sherburn is up to,' he thought, as he stood contemplating the horses walking round in the paddock until the riders were ready to mount.

He saw Sherburn walking across, his top-coat hiding his green jacket, the red cap being a conspicuous object on his head, and determined to 'pump' him. But pumping Morgan Sherburn about his horses' chances was generally similar to endeavouring to draw water out of an empty well.

'Your horse goes queerly in the betting,' said Fred Lostock. 'What sort of a chance has he?'

Morgan Sherburn was in a bad temper, and was about to tell Fred Lostock to mind his own business, when he thought:

'Meddlesome beggar! I'll give him a tip, and I hope he'll take it.' Aloud he said: 'I fancy my horse, and I'm going to try and get back what I lost over the last race. Never mind the market. You ought to know by this time there is nothing to be got out of ring quotations.'

'Thanks,' replied Fred. 'I fancy Snowstorm, but I shall have a saver on The Slogger.'

'I'm sure to beat him. I have owned The Slogger, so I shall make no mistake in that quarter,' said Sherburn.

Fred Lostock backed Snowstorm, but he did not entirely desert The Slogger. Sir Gordon Sefton put his usual modest sum on his own horse, and Dudley Massie, who felt confident of success, had all his Off Chance winnings on his mount.

The manner in which certain big men in the ring were laying against Snowstorm could not fail to attract attention, and more than one of the stewards made remarks about it. The more the public backed Snowstorm, the longer the price some men in the ring offered against him, and the smaller fry, anxious to ' get a bit,' followed their lead. Fred Lostock saw with dismay that Snowstorm, instead of becoming a hot favourite, rapidly went back in the betting.

'Sherburn would never put me on him if it wasn't all right,' he thought ; but he felt uneasy, for Morgan Sherburn was not a man to be trusted in racing matters. He determined to watch the race closely, and see how Sherburn rode his horse.

The course was about three miles, so there

was ample time for the dozen horses to settle down in their places after the flag fell.

At the end of the first mile a couple of horses came to grief, and there was a long gap between the leader and the last pair.

Morgan Sherburn and Dudley Massie were watching each other, and if Massie was anxious to take the measure of Snowstorm, it was equally certain Sherburn meant to get at the form of The Slogger if possible.

It was a muddling race, and the pace was slow. Dudley Massie saw it was time to go on and catch the leaders, so sent The Slogger along, and Sherburn quickly followed him, but did not attempt to pass him.

'He's on it right enough,' thought Fred Lostock, as he watched Snowstorm through his glasses.

Some members of the ring laughed in their sleeves, because they knew different.

'He's a cunning beggar!' said one book-maker. 'Looks like a fair trier, blest if he doesn't! He'll have to take care. If anything happened to The Slogger, he'd have to win.'

There were only two horses in it now, The Slogger in the lead, and Snowstorm a couple of lengths behind. The Slogger blundered slightly, and as Dudley Massie recovered him, one of his stirrup-leathers broke, and he with difficulty retained his seat. Morgan Sherburn saw what had happened, and swore to himself fiercely.

'D—— it all!' he muttered. 'He did me out of the last race when I wanted to win, and he'll let me win this when I don't want to win.'

The bookmakers who had laid heavily against Snowstorm saw with dismay that Sherburn's horse was in front, and that The Slogger was going badly. They did not, however, know the cause, and silent but deep were the imprecations they hurled at Morgan Sherburn. That worthy glanced round to see where The Slogger was, and took a carefully concealed pull at his mount. Snowstorm, however, was in a galloping mood, and, finding it all plain sailing towards the winning-post, was on excellent terms with himself. Morgan Sherburn saw there was no chance of stopping him; his only hope was that, as the pace was not fast, The Slogger would overtake him.

Dudley Massie, minus a stirrup, rode his best to win, but The Slogger, knowing there was something wrong, would not exert himself. It was a near thing at the finish, but Snowstorm won by a couple of lengths, which ought to have been considerably more.

It was a most unsatisfactory race. Morgan Sherburn's horse won, but he lost money on the race, and put several of his bookmaking friends in a hole. As for Dudley Massie, he was sure The Slogger could have won, had he not had the misfortune to break a stirrup-leather.

'It cannot be helped,' said Sir Gordon good-humouredly. 'Have you any idea of Snowstorm's form?'

'The Slogger will beat him in the Grand National,' said Massie. 'I have no doubt about that. I could have won easily if all had gone well in the race.'

Fred Lostock came up smiling, and said :

'I'm sorry you lost, Sir Gordon, but I had a good win. Sherburn told me he thought Snowstorm would win.'

One of the bookmakers, who had laid heavily against Snowstorm, heard the remark, and muttered :

'Sold, by Gad! I shall have to reckon up with Mr. Sherburn over this affair.'

'I'm glad you had a win,' replied Sir Gordon to Fred ; 'but you were lucky to land your wagers. My fellow is sure to beat Snowstorm at Liverpool.'

'Very likely,' said Fred. 'Snowstorm appeared to win easily, all the same.'

12

Although The Slogger lost the race, Dudley Massie was not at all displeased. He knew the horse had run well, and could have gone on for another mile or more.

Sir Gordon's horses were stabled at the St· James's Hotel the night of the races, and Dudley Massie remained there.

Morgan Sherburn found it difficult to explain matters to the bookmakers, but he succeeded at last in convincing them it was not his fault that Snowstorm won.

'But I heard Mr Lostock tell Sir Gordon Sefton that you told him to back Snowstorm,' said the bookmaker who had overheard the remark.

'So I did,' replied Sherburn. 'You don't suppose I'd be such a fool as to give myself away by telling him not to back him ; besides, he's not a particular pal of mine,' he added, with a grin that caused some laughter.

'What chance have you in the Grand National now?' asked a member of the ring.

'I think better of Snowstorm's chance now than I did before the race,' said Sherburn. 'He is sure to beat The Slogger. I held him safe all the way, and could have passed him at any time.'

After a race - meeting Morgan Sherburn

generally remained in the town for the night, and persuaded three or four choice friends of his own class to do likewise. He had to pay expenses, but he thought nothing of this.

On this particular occasion Morgan Sherburn and his friends dined at the Midland Hotel, and, after imbibing the contents of sundry bottles of champagne, sauntered forth into the streets on mischief bent. They tormented un-offending people, and insulted several women who were going peaceably home. One woman retaliated by knocking Morgan Sherburn's hat over his eyes with her umbrella. This he thought a good joke, and laughed boisterously.

' You shall pay me for that, my fair damsel,' he said, and, clasping her round the waist, attempted to kiss her.

The woman screamed and called him a brute, and as he could not manage her single-handed, two of his companions held her while he per-formed the operation. This was more than some passers-by could stand, and the party would have been roughly handled had they not made good their escape.

In the course of time they found themselves opposite the Royal Hotel, and they had more champagne there. Then they went round to the St. James s, and invaded the comfortable private smoking-room where Dudley Massie and four or five more well-known racing men were quietly sitting. Morgan Sherburn at once began passing remarks upon those present, and using bad language to his friends.

'Sherburn is very tight,' said Fred Lostock to Dudley Massie.

'He's a little beast!' replied the latter; 'I wish he'd go. I shall be tempted to knock him down if he says much to me.'

'Don't take any notice of him,' said Fred: 'he'll only make a scene. Fancy that fellow being Ena Sefton's husband.'

'She cannot know what an out-and-out bad lot he really is,' said Massie, 'although she knows quite sufficient by this time.'

'I got even with you on the second race,' said Morgan Sherburn in a thick voice to Massie, who took no notice of his remark, but continued to talk to Fred Lostock. This conduct exasperated Morgan Sherburn, and he said loudly: 'Do you hear me, or are you deaf? You rode a d——d bad race on The Slogger! Stirrup leather broke, did it? Bah! I've known stirrup leathers break before to-day. It's convenient for 'em to break sometimes; gives an excuse for bad riding, or worse.'

The men with him laughed, and Dudley
Massie said angrily :

'If all I hear be true, you were not very
anxious to win on Snowstorm.'

Fred Lostock looked at Massie in amaze-
ment, and whispered :

'You're mistaken, old chap. He told me to
back him.'

'That's a lie!' yelled Morgan Sherburn,
answering Massie.

'Shut up, and make less row, Sherburn,'
growled a man sitting in one corner of the
room. 'You always create a beastly disturbance wherever you are.'

Sherburn turned on the speaker and poured
out a torrent of abuse, but he quieted down
when the man rose to his feet and said firmly :

'If you don't keep quiet, I'll throw you out
of the bar.'

'Lostock backed my horse,' said Sherburn ;
'I told him to back it. Tell your precious
chum what I say is correct.'

'You certainly told me to back your horse,'
said Fred ; 'but I fancy I was lucky to win my
money. Had all gone well with The Slogger,
you might have had to put up with second place.'

'Rubbish!' said Sherburn. 'You had a win
over my horse to-day ; I'll bet you a monkey

Snowstorm beats The Slogger in the Grand National, wherever they finish.'

'I don't want to bet that way,' said Fred. 'I would sooner put five hundred on one straight out.'

'I'll bet you two monkeys to one that Snowstorm beats The Slogger,' said Sherburn.

'Do you mean it?' said Fred.

'Of course I mean it. Will you take it?'

'Yes,' replied Fred. 'A thousand to five hundred you lay me that Snowstorm beats The Slogger in the Grand National?'

'A fool and his money, etc.,' whispered Dudley Massie, but not so low as to escape Morgan Sherburn.

'I'm a fool, am I? We shall see about that. I'll lay you the same odds to a smaller sum, if you wish. I've had one monkey out of you over the fight; I don't suppose you can afford to lose another. I'll oblige you all I can, and throw in Off Chance with The Slogger.'

Dudley Massie could not resist the taunts Sherburn hurled at him again in his usual manner.

'If it will keep your tongue still, I'll accept two hundred to a hundred,' said Massie, 'and take Off Chance in with it.'

Morgan Sherburn booked the wager as well

as he was able, considering the shakiness of
his hand. A telegram fell out of his pocket-
book on to the table, and he saw Dudley
Massie's eyes fasten upon it. He chuckled,
and said, as he picked it up and replaced it in
his book

'You'd like to get hold of that, I'll bet. Not
just yet, my friend. I mean to make use of it
later on.'

Dudley Massie looked savagely at the
speaker, but made no reply ; and Fred Lostock
said :

'What the deuce does he mean ?'

'Oh, it is nothing,' said Dudley Massie.
'Merely a bit of information he imagines may
be of some future use to him.'

When Fred Lostock was going to his bedroom, the bookmaker who overheard his remark
to Sir Gordon Sefton about Sherburn telling
him to back Snowstorm said :

'Good-night, Mr. Lostock. You were lucky
to win on Snowstorm to-day.'

'Why ?' asked Fred, always ready to gain
information.

'Because he was a "dead un," that's all.
Good-night ; and don't put too much faith in
Morgan Sherburn's tips in future,' was the
reply.

CHAPTER XVIII.

MORGAN SHERBURN'S WIFE.

ENA SHERBURN returned from Paris in company
with her maid, as she had no intention of remaining until Morgan Sherburn chose to fetch
her.   As for her husband, he cared but little
whether she remained in Paris or returned to
London.   He meant to go his own way regard-
less of consequences, and quieted what small
amount of conscience he had by saying to
himself :

'I have made a handsome settlement on her,
and she has plenty of money to enjoy herself
with, and that is all women want.   If she plays
her game too strong, I can stop her by using
that telegram.   What a fool Massie was to let
me handle it !   He's in love with Ena, and I
believe she's half inclined to encourage him.
She must remember she is my property, and I
don't care for anything belonging to me to be
damaged and depreciated.'

Ena Sherburn made no further mention of the
telegram, nor of the letter she had written to her
husband, and which Dudley Massie delivered.
Morgan Sherburn was rather surprised at this.
He expected a furious scene, and was half

disappointed it had not come off as he anticipated. His wife treated him coldly, with a
haughty contempt that, under the circumstances,
became her well. Her conduct exasperated her
husband, more especially as he could find no
grounds upon which to pick a quarrel with her.
She answered him when he spoke to her, but
never encouraged conversation with him. She
went her way, and did as she pleased without
consulting him in the least. He never knew
whether she was at home without making
inquiries.

'Madam has gone out driving,' said her
maid. 'She did not say where she was going,
or when she would return, and left no message
for you.'

Morgan Sherburn swore at the maid, and
thought, 'She knows all about it, but has
instructions to say nothing.'

He tried to bribe his wife's maid, and even
went so far as to attempt to flirt with her, but
he was repulsed in a manner he had seldom
been accustomed to. Raymond Daly tried his
blandishments on Rosine—such was the maid's
name—but found it all of no avail. Rosine
snubbed him, and ordered him to keep his
place.

'I have no regard for either you or your

master,' she said. 'I love madam, and she is worth forty such men as you. Bah!' and the smart Rosine snapped her fingers in the valet's face.

'I'll have you turned out of the house,' said Daly angrily.

'*You* will have *me* turned out!' laughed Rosine. 'That is good! It makes me laugh very much to hear you. Have *me* turned out! What a big joke!' and she tripped away, leaving Daly furious as he heard her merriment increasing as she went.

He shook his fist after her, and vowed he would do all in his power to make things unpleasant for her.

'I am having some friends here to-night,' said Morgan Sherburn to his wife one morning as she came into the room to look for something, and he saw she was dressed to go out for her drive.

'Indeed,' she replied. 'You will probably enjoy yourself.'

'I should like you to be present at dinner,' he said.

She looked at him haughtily, and replied:

'Your friends are not my friends, and I decline to entertain men I have not even seen.'

' My friends are good enough for my wife,'
he said.

' Possibly in your opinion, but not in mine,'
she replied.

' You prefer your own friends, no doubt,' he
said.

' I do.'

' Dudley Massie, for instance,' he sneered.

A faint tinge of colour mounted upon Ena's
face, but she controlled her feelings, and
said :

' Mr. Massie is certainly one of my friends.
I do not think he belongs to your set. He is
more particular than you are as to the men he
associates with.'

' Why did you not send another telegram to
him, and ask him to fetch you back from
Paris ?' said. Sherburn. ' He would have
jumped at the chance, and made an admirable
escort.'

' I am not in the habit of sending telegrams
to gentlemen,' said Ena. ' If you allude to the
telegram you ordered to be sent from Paris to
Mr. Massie in my name, you are welcome to
any satisfaction you may derive from such a
despicable action. I am not at all interested in
the matter.'

' But you will be interested when I inform

you I have the telegram in my possession,'
he said.

She started, and for a moment appeared at
a loss what to say. She knew how such a man
as Morgan Sherburn could use the telegram to
her disadvantage. He saw he had scored a
point, and said :

' I think it will be my duty to show the
telegram to your father ; it will put him on his
guard against Massie.'

' The telegram is a forgery. No one will
believe I sent it for a moment. You can do as
you like with it. I am not afraid of you or
your actions. Now I am going out to get a
little fresh air. Your presence seems to pollute
the atmosphere,' said Ena, as she swept out of
the room.

' She is a fine woman,' said Morgan Sherburn,
as he looked at her retreating figure. ' What
a pity she's such a prude ! Now, if she only
had a disposition like Flossie's, we might get
on very well together. I have not had any
ladies to supper since she has been in the
house ; but if she does not change for the
better, I shall have to fall back on some of my
charmers.'

Ena Sherburn's drive was not enjoyable.
Her thoughts were not pleasant companions.

She saw now that the compact she entered into with Morgan Sherburn before her marriage could not be carried out to her satisfaction—in fact, it was unworkable. She hated herself for marrying him, and yet there was no one to blame but herself in the matter.

'If I could only be free again!' she thought; and how many women who have acted as Ena Sherburn have thought the same thing.

'I must be free; I cannot live with this man. A year in his society will make me a different woman. I understand now why so many women lose their self-respect, and console themselves with other admirers. True, I need not have married him, and I hardly know why I did so. If it was to gain wealth and position, I have failed miserably. Wealth I have, but acquiring it from such a source pollutes it, and I have lost position, not gained. I saw what a mistake I had made before I had been married a week—nay, before I had been a wife for twenty-four hours;' and she shuddered.

'I will go down to Sefton,' she thought. 'A change will do me good, and I need not let them know at present how miserably my marriage has turned out.'

Morgan Sherburn had his dinner-party, and his wife, who had gone to the theatre in order to be out of the house, heard the riotous proceedings as she entered the hall.

By an unfortunate chance, Morgan Sherburn
heard, or fancied he heard, his wife return.   He
staggered from the table, and opened the door.
When he saw his wife he laughed, and said :

'I hope you have had a pleasant night.
You see, we are enjoying ourselves, despite
your absence.   Will you join us at our wine ?
We shall feel honoured, I am sure.'

He attempted to bow, and lurched clumsily
forward, stumbling against his wife.

Ena was so thoroughly disgusted that she
pushed him away from her, and he fell sprawling on the floor.   As he fell he clutched at a
flower-stand, and it came down with a crash.
The noise brought several men, more or less
intoxicated, out of the room, and when they
saw their host on the floor, with the broken
flower-vases around him, they laughed at the
ridiculous figure he made.

None of them knew Morgan Sherburn's
wife, and one of the men said :

'Who's the lady—friend of yours, Morgan ?
She's a fine woman.   I admire your taste.'

Ena drew herself up to her full height, and,
with stinging contempt in every tone of her
voice and looks, said

' I am sorry to say I am that man's wife, and therefore I cannot expect his friends to be gentlemen.'

She went up the staircase proudly, and left the men in the hall looking somewhat abashed at Morgan Sherburn, who with assistance got on to his feet and began to abuse his wife in his choicest language. This conduct proved even too much for his friends, who quickly left the house, thinking what an unmitigated cad had entertained them.

Before Morgan Sherburn came down the next morning his wife had left the house with her maid, and was on her way to the Midlands. He came down to breakfast soon after twelve and found a note on the table. He opened it and read :

' I have gone to see my father. If you have any desire to make amends for your disgraceful conduct of last night, do not follow me to Sefton. At least, let me have a few days to myself where I shall not be troubled with your society.'

There was no signature.

He crushed the letter in his hand, threw it on the ground and stamped upon it, picked up a boot and hurled it at the fox-terrier on the hearth, and then stamped about the room, trying to exhaust his rage.

The cool, contemptuous way in which his wife treated him made him wild. He would have preferred her to storm at him and get into a terrible passion.

He thought how he could annoy her, and decided that if he followed her to Sefton it would be the best way of accomplishing that end.

'I'll go down to-morrow,' he muttered, 'and take Daly with me. That will be a double source of annoyance to her. She hates Daly almost as much as she hates me. I'll wire to Sir Gordon that I am coming. That will take the wind out of her sails. She's too proud to complain to her people about me. If she turns nasty when I am there, I'll show that telegram to Sir Gordon. That will explain to him why I did not return to Paris for her.'

He rang the bell, and Raymond Daly appeared.

'Send a telegram to Sir Gordon Sefton, and say I shall be at Sefton House to-morrow.'

'Yes, sir,' replied Daly. 'Mrs. Sherburn left this morning for Sefton.'

'How do you know?' said Sherburn.

'Her maid informed me; and said how

delighted she was to get away from such a disgraceful house,' replied Daly.

'Oh, she said that, did she?' growled Sherburn; 'and what did you say?'

'I told her to go——'

'Oh yes, I know where,' said his master; 'and I wish she would take your advice. She's a nasty little spitfire; but I'll have it stopped, or out she goes.'

'The sooner the better,' said Daly. 'It is not safe to leave things about with that girl in the house.'

'Oh, shut up with that humbug,' said Sherburn; 'you're not so particular yourself. The girl is honest enough, but she has too much of her own way.'

Daly went out in high ill-humour.

'So you think I'm not honest,' he muttered. 'I shall know how to take care of myself in future.'

Considering that Raymond Daly had been feathering his nest ever since he had been in Morgan Sherburn's service, the remark was superfluous.

Her parents were not much surprised when Ena arrived at Sefton House, and she made no excuse for her unexpected visit, only to say that she wanted to be out of London until the spring set in.

13

Arthur Sefton, however, hinted to Beatrice that there was something wrong, and he should not be at all surprised if she had given Morgan Sherburn the slip.

Beatrice was shocked, and said he must not hint at such things. When Sir Gordon received Morgan Sherburn's telegram, he said to Ena

'Your husband wires he is coming down to-morrow. You see, he cannot bear to be parted from you for more than a day.'

Ena expected this, but she was annoyed at the thought of Morgan Sherburn coming to Sefton. She knew, however, he would have to behave himself during his stay at her father's house, and this consoled her somewhat.

CHAPTER XIX.

WHAT SIR GORDON OVERHEARD.

'MORGAN SHERBURN is coming to-day,' said Arthur Sefton to Dudley Massie, who had come up to the house to wheel the crippled lad down to the stables. 'I wish to goodness he would keep away. It is bad enough to have Ena in the house again. Oh, I forgot : you did not know Ena arrived yesterday. It's my opinion she's had a quarrel with that blessed husband of hers, and that she came here to give him the slip. Morgan evidently does not wish to part with her at present, so he is coming in pursuit. He'd better keep out of my way, or I shall say something nasty to him. Don't you go fooling around Ena now she is here. Take my advice and keep out of her way. She is dangerous—all good-looking women are, especially when they are married.'

'You are in a lecturing humour this morning,' said Dudley Massie. 'If Mr. Sherburn arrives to-day, you are not likely to see much of him. I hope he will not interfere about the horses.'

'The governor will stand no interference,' said Arthur; 'you may depend upon that. Ever since Derby races he seems to have changed his opinion of Morgan. I don't think he ever cared for him much, and he cares less now.'

Dudley Massie met Ena Sherburn before her husband arrived, and had a few minutes' conversation with her.

'It was unwise of you to allow my husband to obtain that telegram,' she said.

'I am very sorry I handed it to him,' said

Dudley. 'I tried to get it back, and should have done so, but he had a couple of men to help him, and I could not do anything against three of them.'

'He may make use of it,' said Ena. 'I must try and obtain possession of it.'

'It is a forgery,' said Dudley; 'and you can easily explain that you did not send it. Why not tell your father about it?'

'I would rather not,' said Ena. 'I cannot prove who did send it, although I have no doubt myself.'

As they were talking together, Sir Gordon Sefton came up with Beatrice, and the latter seemed surprised to see her sister alone with Dudley Massie.

'Are you trying to worm stable secrets from Ena?' laughed Sir Gordon. 'You will have more chance with her than I shall have with Morgan. By the way, he arrives this afternoon. I must try and find out what he means to do over the Grand National, and what chance he thinks Snowstorm has now'

'I overheard him remark that he thought Snowstorm would win,' said Ena; 'but I am not at all interested in it. I would much rather see your horse win, father.'

'And I hope you will have that pleasure,'

said Sir Gordon. 'Now you are here, you may as well remain and go to Liverpool with us.'

'I will remain here if you will have me,' said Ena ; 'but I have not much inclination to go to Liverpool at present. Do you ride The Slogger, Mr. Massie ?'

'I hope to have that pleasure,' said Dudley. 'If Off Chance improves with another gallop or two, I shall hardly know which to ride.'

'You are becoming prejudiced in favour of Off Chance, since he won at Derby,' said Sir Gordon. 'For my part, I do not think it will be wise to run them both.'

Dudley Massie could not help thinking of what Arthur Sefton had said to him as he looked at Beatrice, and he wondered if it could be true that she was not indifferent to him. As he looked at her Beatrice caught his glance, and her face went a rosy red, and she cast down her eyes in some confusion. Beatrice was very fond of Dudley Massie, but she took great care to conceal her feelings. Ena had seen the glance that passed between them, and noticed how her sister betrayed herself. She felt angry with Beatrice and also with Dudley Massie, although she had no right to be so.

'Beatrice is in love with him,' she thought, 'and she cannot conceal the fact, much as she tries to do so. I must warn her not to plant her affections in an uncongenial soil. Dudley Massie is not in love with her, of that I am sure.'

When Morgan Sherburn arrived, Ena lost no time in seeing him alone.

'Why have you followed me down here?' she asked.

'Why did you leave me behind?' he replied.

'You know well enough why I came away. I was grossly insulted by some of your friends the night before I left, and I did not care to remain longer in the house,' she said.

'I presume you will return to the house,' he said.

'When it suits my convenience,' replied Ena.

'And I shall remain here until you agree to return with me,' he said.

'You will remain some time, then,' she said. 'I have arranged to remain here and accompany my father to Liverpool to see the Grand National.'

'Oh, that's the arrangement, is it?' said Morgan Sherburn; 'and I have not been consulted at all. Supposing I object to the arrangement?'

'That will not alter my plans,' said Ena.

'But you have not answered my question. Why did you follow me here?'

'Because I could not bear to be parted from you,' he replied. 'I am so very proud of you, I dare not trust you out of my sight. Besides, it is dangerous for you to be here, and I wish to shield you from the attentions of Mr. Massie.'

'How dare you talk to me like this!' she said. 'Mr. Massie is nothing to me, and you know it. If you insult me again, I shall tell my father that one of us must leave the house.'

The door of Morgan Sherburn's room was partly open, and as Sir Gordon Sefton passed, he could not help overhearing Ena's words. He hesitated as to whether he should make his presence known or pass on. Before he had decided, Ena came out of the room, and she saw by Sir Gordon's face he had overheard her words.

'You heard what I said?' she asked.

'Yes,' replied her father; 'I was passing at the time, and, as the door was partly open and you spoke in rather a loud tone of voice, I could not help hearing.'

'Then perhaps you will step inside, and I will explain,' she said, and held the door wide open for him.

There was nothing for it but to step into the room, although Sir Gordon would have much preferred not to do so.

'My father heard my remark accidentally,' said Ena to her husband. 'I wish to explain to him that you have thought fit to couple my name on more than one occasion with that of Mr. Massie. Why you have done so is best known to yourself.'

'I am surprised at this, Sherburn,' said Sir Gordon. 'I certainly did not expect you to insult my daughter when you married her. I cannot permit you to do so, and I think you ought to apologize.'

'When you know all the facts, Sir Gordon, you will not ask me to apologize. I have good grounds for all I have said. If your daughter allows her feelings to get the better of her dis- cretion, she is to blame for it, not I,' said Morgan Sherburn.

'Do you mean to insinuate that my daughter entertains feelings for Mr. Massie that she has no right to do?' said Sir Gordon angrily.

'As you have put it so plainly, that is just about what I do mean,' said Sherburn coolly. 'The only difference is that I might have put it in more forcible language.'

Sir Gordon Sefton looked at Ena, and she said ·

'This is only one of the many insults I have had to submit to during my brief married life. It was not your fault I married this man. I was free to choose for myself, and I now acknowledge I made a fatal mistake. Had I taken your advice, I should have been much happier.'

'So you advised her not to marry me,' said Morgan Sherburn. 'Much obliged to you, I am sure. I also wish she had taken your advice. It was hardly a fair bargain for me to settle a large sum of money on her when she was all the time in love with another man.'

'Many more words such as these, and I shall forget you are my son-in-law, and that I am your host,' said Sir Gordon with dignity. 'You have no shadow of proof upon which to make such accusations, and it is contemptible in you to make them, even if they were true.'

'No proof?' said Morgan Sherburn. 'Ask my wife if I have no proof.'

'I will not!' said Sir Gordon. 'Ena is my child, and I would trust her honour as I would my own.'

She thanked him with a look, and Morgan Sherburn, exasperated, said :

'I have in my possession a telegram my wife sent from Paris to Mr. Massie, asking him to meet her there during my absence in London.'

'That is not true,' said Ena. 'He has a telegram purporting to be sent by me, but it is a forgery. I never sent any such telegram.'

Morgan Sherburn took the telegram out of his pocket-book, and said

'You can read this, Sir Gordon. Seeing is believing.'

He spread it out on the table, and Sir Gordon Sefton read it.

'Did you send this telegram to Mr. Massie?' he asked Ena.

'No,' she replied; 'I sent him no telegram.'

'Do you know who did send it?'

'No.'

'But you suspect someone?'

'Yes.'

'Who?'

'I would rather not say. I have no proof, but I believe my surmise to be correct.'

'Did Mr. Massie receive this telegram?' asked Sir Gordon.

'He did,' said Ena.

'Did he visit you in Paris in response to it?'

'Yes; and I respect him for doing so. He

once promised me, if I needed a friend, he would
do all in his power to help me. Knowing what
my husband's true character is, he probably
thought the telegram genuine, and came to my
assistance,' said Ena.

'And what does he think of it?'' said Sir
Gordon.

'He knows I did not send it, and that I was
very much surprised to see him in Paris,' said
Ena.

'Why have you not told me of this before?'
said Sir Gordon.

'Because she dared not!' said Morgan Sherburn. 'She did send this telegram, and she
has confessed that Mr. Massie visited her in
Paris. What more do you want?'

'Much more!' said Sir Gordon Sefton,
turning sharply round and facing Morgan
Sherburn, who shrank back from him. 'I
want to know who sent this telegram, and I
will find out. I respect my daughter for concealing her suspicions, but I do not fail to see
in which direction they point. I mean to get
at the bottom of this miserable business. As
her husband, you ought to have taken steps in
this direction at once. Why did you not do
so?'

'Because I thought it better, for her sake,

that publicity should not be given to the affair,'
said Sherburn.

' Do you doubt my daughter's honour, sir ?'
asked Sir Gordon angrily.

Bad as he was, Morgan Sherburn felt he
could not tell such a dastardly lie as to answer
in the affirmative.

Sir Gordon repeated his question, and Sherburn said

' No, I do not doubt her honour, but she has
been guilty of a very grave indiscretion.'

' She denies all knowledge of that telegram,'
said Sir Gordon.

' I cannot believe her,' said Morgan Sherburn.

' I believe her,' said Sir Gordon, ' and you
ought to be the first to believe in your wife.   I
am very sorry for you, Sherburn.   How can
you expect Ena to believe in you when you act
in this manner ?   I shall say no more about the
matter while you remain here ; I shall not
mention it to Lady Sefton, and I desire you
not to do so.   How long do you intend to
remain ?'

The question was put in such a manner that
Morgan Sherburn could not fail to understand
that Sir Gordon wished him to go as soon as
possible.

'I must return to-morrow,' he said. 'I have some important business connected with the Grand National to attend to. Shall you be ready to go back with me?' he added, looking at Ena.

'My daughter has decided to remain here and accompany us to Liverpool,' said Sir Gordon. 'I hope you have no objections.'

'Not if you wish it,' replied Morgan Sherburn.

'Come, Ena,' said Sir Gordon; 'I wish to speak to you alone.'

Left to himself, Morgan Sherburn gave way to one of his usual fits of temper. He had been worsted again in his endeavour to cast aspersion upon his wife, and he knew he deserved all he had got and more. This only added fuel to the flame, and made him more determined than ever to lower Ena's pride and humble her in the dust. He cared naught for truth or honesty, and his code of honour, if he ever possessed one, was smashed to atoms. He vowed vengeance against the whole Sefton family and Dudley Massie. He knew they despised him, and also suspected the truth about the telegram; but he had the telegram in his possession, and there were others who would be only too ready to believe its contents.

Ena Sherburn was not a woman to make friends amongst her own sex. She was haughty and independent, and this made her many enemies. There is nothing some women like more than pulling the character of one of their own sex to pieces, scattering them broadcast before the world. Morgan Sherburn knew certain society ladies who cordially hated his wife. The possession of such a telegram to these ladies would be looked upon as a stroke of exceeding good-fortune. It would enable them to retaliate upon Ena Sherburn for the snubbing she had rightly put upon them. Morgan Sherburn's money bought these ladies' favours, and he paid dearly for them. Women who have lost self-respect and honour, no matter in what society they may move, hate to see in some good woman a reflection of their lives before their fall, and wish to shatter the mirror that puts them to shame. Men like Sherburn find in such women ready tools.

CHAPTER XX.

THE BREACH WIDENS.

LADY BETTY PORTSDOWN had an accommodating husband, some years older than herself, who took but little notice of her ladyship's doings. He married her because he considered her clever and pretty, and he had arrived at an age when beauty's smiles are not often bestowed upon such men. Lord Portsdown was a poor man, having spent all the ready money he could lay hands on in his bachelor days, and he had mortgaged all the property he could possibly raise loans upon. This did not prevent his living in an extravagant style in town, owning a few racehorses, and gambling heavily. When there was a young 'pigeon' to be plucked, ' Porty '—as his familiars called him—generally secured some of the best feathers.

Lady Betty came of a good old family, and her brother and her two elder sisters were grieved and ashamed at her behaviour. If the truth must be told, Lady Betty married Lord Portsdown because she wished to escape from certain entanglements in another direction. She had received the cut direct from many

well-known people, and the worst cut of all
came from Ena Sherburn.

Before her marriage Lady Betty had been
introduced to Ena Sefton, and when she heard
of her marriage with Morgan Sherburn she
was amused. Hearing Ena was in Paris, Lady
Betty called upon her. Mrs. Sherburn received
her, but plainly gave her to understand she
had no desire to continue the acquaintance.

Lady Betty was not the woman to forgive
slights of this description, and she determined
to return what she considered Mrs. Sherburn's
insult in full. She had been on intimate terms
with Morgan Sherburn for some time. People
wondered if her husband was blind to her
follies, or worse, for her conduct with Morgan
Sherburn was notorious. Lady Betty bled
Sherburn freely, and Lord Portsdown found
this rich young man's money very useful.

'Get what you can out of him,' was Portsdown's advice to his wife; 'but remember I
want my share, or I shall be very nasty.'

'You shall have your share,' said Lady
Betty; 'but remember I am not to be interfered with.'

Lady Betty was just the woman to obtain a
hold over a man like Morgan Sherburn. She
was unscrupulous, and cared very little what

people thought or said about her, so long as they received her at their houses. She was a bold, good-looking, dashing woman, without a conscience or a spark of honour.

It was to Lady Betty that Morgan Sherburn went on his return from Sefton House. He was a welcome visitor, the more so as he was unexpected.

'I thought you had reformed since your marriage,' she said, 'and that you had deserted all your old friends. I have not seen you since you joined the married ranks. Allow me to congratulate you upon having secured such a beautiful and proper wife.'

'I could not have you, Lady Betty, so I had to look elsewhere,' he replied.

'I like you very well as you are,' she said. 'Perhaps if you had married me we should not have been such excellent friends. We are to remains friends, I suppose? Your marriage will make no difference in our amicable relations?'

'Certainly not,' he said. 'I have come to you for consolation, Betty.'

'What!' she exclaimed. 'Not quarrelled already? Why, you have only been married a few weeks. Has she found you out?' and Lady Betty laughed merrily.

'I hardly understand what you mean by

14

finding me out,' he said; 'but I have found her out.'

'This is interesting, most instructive,' said Lady Betty. 'Now, if you had kicked over the traces I could have understood it, but such a perfect woman as your wife—well, really, I am shocked.'

'I am no worse than other men,' growled Sherburn.

'No, my dear; you are very much better than the ordinary run of men; at all events, I think so,' said Lady Betty

'I have been pretty constant to you,' said Sherburn. 'We have been real good pals.'

'We have,' laughed Lady Betty. 'What jolly times we have had! Heigho! they are all over now.'

'All over! Why?' asked Sherburn.

'Why, you stupid man, because you are married. I could never go about with a married man it would be too dreadful.'

'But you were married when I became acquainted with you,' said Sherburn.

'Ah, that is different,' said Lady Betty.

'I don't see it,' he said.

'And I cannot explain,' she replied. 'It is purely a woman's way of reasoning, and you would not understand it. But what have you two turtle-doves quarrelled about? You have not informed me at present. I hope it is not serious.'

'But it is serious,' said Morgan Sherburn. He did not know Lady Betty had called upon his wife in Paris. Had he known, he would have been surprised at her ladyship's shamelessness. 'She has fled to her father's house as a kind of haven of refuge from me. The beauty of it is, she is at fault, not I.'

Lady Betty laughed, a taunting, rippling little laugh of unbelief.

'Don't you believe me?' he asked sharply.

'Now, please keep your temper, Morgan. You are such a bear when you lose your temper. I am quite ready to believe anything you may tell me. You know what implicit confidence I have in you.'

'Bosh!' he said savagely. 'You can believe me or not, but I have proofs.'

'Proofs of what?' asked Lady Betty, thoroughly interested.

'That my wife is in love with another man, and has seen him alone since our marriage. She had the audacity to send for him to Paris during my absence,' said Sherburn.

'During the honeymoon?' said Lady Betty. 'I can hardly believe it.'

14—2

'It is true.   I came to London on business and left her there, and no sooner is my back turned than she sends a telegram to an old admirer to visit her.'

'I didn't think she had it in her,' thought Lady Betty admiringly.   Aloud she said 'What shameful conduct! but are you quite sure she sent for him?'

Morgan Sherburn drew out his pocket-book and took out the telegram.   He handed it to Lady Betty and said :

'Read that.'

She read it, and her eyes flashed.

'Now I can repay her for insulting me,' she thought.   'I must keep this telegram.'

'Have you any doubts now?' asked Sherburn.

'None,' replied Lady Betty.   'The telegram is quite sufficient.   How did it come into your possession?'

'I took it from the man it was sent to.   He taunted me with it, and I got possession of it.'

'Who is Dudley Massie?'

'He is her father's trainer, manager, gentleman jockey, and what not,' said Sherburn.

Lady Betty was radiant with delight.   She could crush her enemy now.

'You seem pleased at my misfortune,' said Sherburn.

' Because I 'shall not lose you,' she said softly.

She knew how to handle Morgan Sherburn, and she wished to retain possession of the telegram.

' Please give me the telegram,' said Sherburn.

' Let me keep it, Morgan,' she said, with one of her most languishing smiles.

' No,' he replied firmly. 'I must have it. I may have occasion to make use of it.'

' Why have you shown me this telegram, and told me this story?' asked Lady Betty.

' Because I thought you would sympathize with me,' he replied.

' That is not correct. You wish to pay your wife out for her neglect of you. That is why you showed me this telegram,' said Lady Betty.

' And if that is my reason, what then?'

' You want my help,' said Lady Betty. ' I am to circulate this interesting news.'

' Well,' said Morgan Sherburn, ' you women are fond of scandal.'

' Not half as fond of it as you men. There are not many women would try and blast their husband's good name as you are trying to do that of your wife.'

Lady Betty, bad as she was, despised

Morgan Sherburn for what he was doing. She felt uneasy now she knew what he was capable of.

'Don't preach to me,' he said. 'I have given you something to talk about, and you ought to be grateful.'

She still held the telegram in her hand, and he again asked her to return it.

'Why not leave it in my possession?' she said. 'If I wish to relate the indiscretion of your wife to my friends, I ought to have some proof.'

'You need no proof. They will be only too ready to believe you,' he said.

'Well, if you must have it, here it is,' said Lady Betty, handing it to him. 'I can say I have seen the telegram, at any rate.'

'I should not do so,' said Sherburn. 'They will ask where you saw it.'

'You are right,' she said : 'it will be better not to mention it.'

Morgan Sherburn remained late at Portsdown's house, and on the return home of Lady Betty's husband towards the small hours he did not seem at all surprised to find Sherburn there.

Lady Betty was not long in circulating the information she had received from Morgan Sherburn. She and her friends gloated over

the supposed fall from the paths of virtue of
Morgan Sherburn's wife. They held up their
hands in pious horror, and declared such conduct was positively shocking.

'And how does Mr. Sherburn take it?' asked
one lady, who had gone through the divorce
court and married again. 'You and he are
such very good friends, my dear Lady Betty.'

Lady Betty looked daggers at the speaker at
this home-thrust.

'Mr. Sherburn is very much upset, naturally,
as he does not wish to have his name bandied
about in the divorce court.'

This was a sharp retort, and the lady wished
she had remained silent. Lady Betty had a
sharp, venomous tongue, as some of her acquaintances knew to their cost.

The scandal spread as fast as a plague : it
multiplied and increased as it was passed on
from one person to another, until many people
heard that Morgan Sherburn's wife had run
away with Sir Gordon Sefton's groom during
her honeymoon. The viler a slander, the more
it appears to flourish ; and even when the
slanderer is unearthed and exposed, there is a
deep wound left behind that seldom entirely
heals. If the Lady Bettys of modern society
knew what misery they cause, they might

hesitate before slandering their neighbours. A second-rate society paper got hold of the scandal, and duly retailed it out to the public at a modest sum. No names were mentioned, but there was no mistaking the hints conveyed. Sir Gordon Sefton saw the paper and the paragraph. A member of his club in London happened to see it, and thinking it would interest his friend Sir Gordon, sent it to him, marking the objectionable lines in red ink, so that there would be no danger of the postage or the paper being wasted. This amiable friend of Sir Gordon's glowed with pleasure and pride at the bare idea of doing such a noble action as he dropped the ' rag ' into the newspaper-box at the club.

Ena Sherburn heard nothing of all this scandal which had accumulated about her in the course of a few days. Sir Gordon Sefton, however, heard of it from more than one source, and his blood boiled at the insults put upon his daughter. He took the offending paper and pointed out the paragraph to Dudley Massie, who felt inclined to rush off to London, thrash the editor, and then seek out Morgan Sherburn.

' This must be put a stop to,' said Sir Gordon; ' but how to do it without further publicity ? That must be avoided, if possible.'

' I hope Mrs. Sherburn knows nothing of these vile slanders,' said Massie.

' She does not at present, but she will do so when she returns to town,' said Sir Gordon. ' Do you really believe Sherburn caused that telegram to be sent? I can hardly believe any man capable of such an action.'

' I feel certain he had it sent,' said Dudley.

' By Heaven, if I find out such to be the case,' said Sir Gordon, ' I will horsewhip him in public, son-in-law or no son-in-law.'

' He will deserve all he receives,' said Dudley. ' I shall have an account to settle with him, too. I must wait until after next week. The race will be over then, and I shall not be afraid of anything that may happen. I do not wish to do anything that may prevent either Sherburn or myself riding.'

' Quite right,' said Sir Gordon. ' I have perfect faith in Ena, and I can wait until the proper time arrives to retaliate. When that time does come, Morgan Sherburn will find he is in a very nasty tight place.'

CHAPTER XXI.

AT LIVERPOOL.

THE SLOGGER'S preparation for the Grand National was finished, and the winding-up gallop had been in every respect satisfactory. Dudley Massie was sanguine of pulling off the big event at Aintree, and his spirits, which had been depressed on account of the scandals afloat, rose considerably. Dudley Massie always took care of himself, and was generally fit to ride a severe race. It was not so with Morgan Sherburn, who was inclined to put on weight, and did not lead a steady life. Turkish-baths and sundry 'doses' were necessary to bring down his weight, and they weakened him and undermined his constitution.

There had been some heavy wagering on the Grand National, and Sherburn's horse was well backed. Additional interest attached to the event because a couple of Australian horses were to run in it.

When Dudley Massie arrived in Liverpool he went to the Adelphi Hotel, where Sir Gordon Sefton had engaged rooms for his party. Morgan Sherburn had the bad taste to select the same hotel, and his rooms were adjoining those of the Seftons.

Dudley Massie avoided him as much as possible, for he felt he might do something rash if Sherburn taunted him.

The morning after he arrived in Liverpool, Dudley Massie met Fred Bexley, the horse-dealer from whom he bought The Slogger. Bexley was a well-known man in hunting and turf circles, and managed to obtain a good deal of varied information. The horse-dealer liked Dudley Massie, and had a particular aversion to Morgan Sherburn. He welcomed Dudley cordially, and said

'I see The Slogger is well backed for the National. I knew he was a good one when I sold him you, but I hardly expected him to win a National, or you would not have got him for that price. You ride him, of course?'

'Yes, I ride him, and he has a good chance,' said Dudley. 'Have you heard much about the race?'

'A lot, one way or another,' said Bexley. 'We hear a heap of talk at our place, and I travel about a good deal. I was over in Ireland a week or so back, and there is a horse called Donnybrook they fancy very much.'

'I heard he was a good one,' said Dudley;

'and he comes out of a dangerous stable. Kavanagh rides him, I think, and he's a good horseman.'

'I hear Sherburn is trying to buy Donny-brook,' said Bexley, 'but they are holding out for a stiff price.'

'Then he cannot have such a great opinion of Snowstorm,' said Dudley.

'You have no occasion to be afraid of Snow-storm,' said Bexley; 'you may take my tip for that. If Snowstorm wins a National, I shall be very much surprised. It is odds on The Slogger beating him. I know both horses well, and I'd bet on that.'

'Sherburn laid two to one on Snowstorm beating The Slogger at Derby,' said Dudley. 'He laid Fred Lostock a thousand to five hundred, and me two hundred to a hundred, and gave me Off Chance in.'

'Then he's a fool!' said Bexley; 'and Lostock has secured a very good wager.'

'There is sure to be a big field,' said Dudley. 'I hear about twenty-five or thirty runners.'

'Too many,' said Bexley; 'and more than half of them have no chance. They cause a lot of damage, those bad horses, and interfere with the good ones. You will have your work cut out to steer a clear course if there are so many runners.'

'I have ridden over Aintree before,' said Dudley, 'and know my way well; but, as you say, it is a difficult matter to steer clear in such a big field.'

'Will Sir Gordon start Off Chance?' asked Bexley.

'Yes; and I thought he had more than an "off chance," until our last trial, when The Slogger gave him a " big doing."'

'I can find Sir Gordon a customer for Off Chance, if he cares to sell,' said Bexley.

'He will not sell him before the race; but I will ask him to put a price on afterwards,' said Dudley.

'I suppose you are not afraid of Sherburn playing you any tricks in the race?' asked Bexley. 'He's a nasty beggar when he's riled.'

'He had better not try it on,' said Dudley. 'I know he is not particular, and I have seen him jostle a horse and bring him down more than once. If he attempts that with me, I shall cut him over the face with my whip, and he'll bear the mark to remind him of it for a long time.'

'From all accounts, he has good grounds for hating you,' said Bexley.

'Why; what have you heard?' asked
Dudley.

'Mind, I don't believe all I hear,' said Bexley.
'I should never be able to make ends meet in
my trade if I did.   I have heard it said that
you are rather too thick with Mrs. Sherburn,
and that she is more partial to your society
than her husband's.   I'm not surprised at that;
but then she's married, and it does not do to
neglect husbands.'

'There is not a word of truth in what you
have heard,' said Dudley.   'The author of
these slanders will be punished severely before
long.   Sir Gordon Sefton would not place
confidence in me if these accusations were true.
He knows they are vile slanders, and he will
protect his daughter from them.'

'I always said it was a parcel of lies,' said
Bexley; 'but you know how people will talk,
and there is a certain amount of sympathy for
Sherburn.   By the way, do you know Lady
Betty Portsdown?   She is a great friend of
Morgan Sherburn's.   I know Lord Portsdown.
He's an awful old rake.   He told me about
Mrs. Sherburn and yourself, and said his wife
gave him the information.'

'I know Lady Betty by reputation,' said
Dudley, 'and, from all I hear, she is a bad lot.

A woman like that would take a delight in slandering Mrs. Sherburn.'

'I believe you, my boy,' said Bexley. 'Some people say she ought to be Mrs. Sherburn, and, by Gad! I dare say they are right. Her husband is a regular sharper; I can call him by no other name. Such men ought to be shot.'

'I know very little about Portsdown,' said Dudley; 'and what I do know does not redound to his credit.'

'He has a horse in the National,' said Bexley, 'and it is backed at outside prices.'

'Any chance?' asked Dudley.

'No. I sold it him,' said Bexley, with a wink.

Dudley Massie laughed as he said

'It was wrong of you to take advantage of Lord Portsdown's ignorance.'

'He thought he knew more about it than I did, so I let him have his own way. Portsdown has a very good opinion of himself, and considers he is an excellent judge of a horse. Those are the men I like as customers. You can always get rid of something you do not want to them.'

Dudley Massie had not long left Bexley when he came across Fred Lostock.

'What's all this talk about Mrs. Sherburn and yourself?' asked Fred.

'So you have heard it!' said Dudley Massie angrily; 'and I suppose you believe it?'

'I beg your pardon,' said Lostock, 'I do not believe a word of it. I had a row with Portsdown about it last night. I told him it was a beastly shame, and didn't reflect credit on the scandalmongers who had circulated it. He fired up and said he got his information from his wife, and that Mr. Sherburn had told Lady Betty about it. That staggered me for a moment, but I recovered and fired off at Porty in a style he least expected. I told him if he would look after his own wife and leave the doings of other men's wives alone, it would redound more to his credit. The old heathen was furious, and I piled on the agony by saying, if there was any trouble in the divorce court, it would be Morgan Sherburn and a very near relation of Porty's who would suffer the most damage. I fought a right royal battle for you, old fellow, but you do not seem a bit grateful.'

'It was very good of you to speak out your mind,' said Dudley. 'What I regret is that there should be any occasion for you to do so. Portsdown I believe is about in the same class as Sherburn.'

'Worse, my boy, worse,' said Fred. 'Porty is a disgrace to our sex. There are no depths of infamy that he cannot bottom. I hope he will sink deep into those depths and never come out before long, because there is no chance of his reforming.'

'Let us drop the unsavoury subject,' said Dudley. 'Come and have a glass of wine with me.' They went into the Comptor and sat down for a few minutes. 'You have a good bet with Sherburn, according to Bexley,' said Dudley. 'I met him this morning, just before I came across you, and he says The Slogger is sure to beat Snow-storm.'

'I'm glad of that,' said Fred. 'Bexley is a good judge, and I'm not too flush of ready money. I should not like to lose five hundred to Sherburn, of all men in the world.'

'Bexley says there is a horse called Donny-brook has a chance, and that Sherburn is trying to buy him.'

'Then he may as well spare himself the trouble,' said Fred; 'I know the horse is not for sale. A particular friend of mine from over the water owns him, and there is no fear of his parting with him. Take my tip, and keep a sharp eye on Donnybrook in the race, for he will be one of the hardest to beat. When the Irishmen put their money down on a Grand

National candidate, you may safely bet there is danger in that quarter.'

'They do not make many mistakes,' said Dudley ; 'and most of those Irish horses are born jumpers. I think there's some Irish blood in The Slogger.'

A well-known steeplechase-rider named O'Hara came into the room, and, seeing Dudley Massie and Fred Lostock, stepped across to them.

'Well, Jim, over here again ?' said Dudley. 'What do you ride in the National ?'

'My luck's dead out,' said the jockey 'We had a fair chance with Eileen, but she's gone lame, and I have no mount.'

'Here's a chance,' thought Dudley, 'to secure him for Off Chance. I know Dixon will not mind standing down for him, and Jim O'Hara is a real good man.'

'I think I can find you a mount, Jim,' said Dudley. 'Sir Gordon Sefton has two horses in the race. I ride The Slogger, and Dixon is at present on Off Chance ; but I know he would not mind standing down for you. I should much prefer to see you up if you will accept the mount, on the condition Sir Gordon agrees to it.'

'Has the horse a chance ?' asked O'Hara.

' A good rough outside chance,' said Dudley.
' A week ago I put him down as better than
The Slogger. He'll carry you well, and get
the country. You'll have a nice safe ride, any
way.'

' I don't care about looking at the race; I
would sooner be in it on anything decent,' said
O'Hara.

' I will see Sir Gordon about it as soon as I
reach home,' said Dudley. ' May I tell him
you will accept the mount ?'

' Yes, on conditions I am not to sacrifice Off
Chance to your mount if I think he can win,'
said O'Hara.

' You may beat me if you can, Jim,' said
Dudley ; ' but, mind, I do not think you have
much chance of doing so unless something
happens.'

' There's always that chance in a race like
the National,' said O'Hara. ' A horse that
jumps well, even if he is a bit slow, has a good
chance.'

' You will not find Off Chance slow,' said
Dudley. ' The question is as to whether he
will stay the course. He's only four years
old.'

' Is it the horse that won the Juvenile Plate
at Derby?' asked O'Hara.

'Yes,' said Dudley; 'and I rode him in that race. He beat Mr. Sherburn's horse badly.'

'I've heard he is a decent horse,' said Jim. 'It would be rather a joke if my chance mount beat yours.'

'I don't wish you bad luck,' said Fred Lostock; 'but I hope to see The Slogger win.'

'It will not matter about his winning so far as your bet with Sherburn is concerned,' said Dudley. 'You backed The Slogger to beat Snowstorm wherever they finished.'

'So I did,' replied Fred. 'All the better for me.'

When Dudley Massie reached the Adelphi Hotel he lost no time in asking Sir Gordon if Jim O'Hara could have the mount on Off Chance.

'Certainly,' said Sir Gordon. 'I am glad you have found such a good man. Dixon only had the mount in case I could not find a better jockey.'

Dudley Massie sent a message to Jim O'Hara stating Sir Gordon Sefton engaged him to ride Off Chance; and the jockey was pleased to think he had a mount in the race he loved best of all to ride in.

CHAPTER XXII.

IN AINTREE PADDOCK.

AINTREE and the Grand National—what glorious memories of the past these two names conjure up before us! How many great battles have been fought out over the famous steeplechase course on Aintree meadows. The names of Emblem, The Lamb, The Colonel, and, later on, Austerlitz, Shifnal, Woodbrooke, Liberator, and many others, are familiar to all racing men. Hardly a Grand National has been run that does not possess some peculiar interest, or is not connected with some exciting event. Beecher's Brook holds the record as a jump with a world-wide celebrity. There is no sport so exciting and full of interest as steeplechasing, and no cross-country race more fraught with vast results than the Grand National. It is the height of every gentleman rider's ambition to steer a Grand National winner to victory, and find his name enrolled amongst the famous riders who have accomplished the feat. The rider of the Grand National winner is the hero of the hour at Liverpool Spring Meeting. He is the cynosure of all eyes, and his name is on every tongue. The rider of such a winner must possess courage and coolness, and be master of all those resources that make a man stand out conspicuously amongst his fellows.

Small wonder, then, that Dudley Massie, as he stood in the paddock at Aintree and thought over all these things, felt a fierce determination rise in him to ride The Slogger to victory if possible. For a few moments he was alone, and he occupied the time in thinking how he ought to ride in order to win on The Slogger. He knew the horse had peculiarities. The Slogger had more than once shown Dudley Massie that he wanted to be master instead of his rider, if possible. They had fierce fights together during The Slogger's training, and were all the better friends for it. Dudley Massie knew he must be the master on every occasion, or there would be no chance of making The Slogger do his best.

As the time approached for the great race to be decided he felt anxious, but he lost none of his coolness and determination. He glanced round the paddock, and saw many men he knew and also some ladies. Dudley Massie was a popular gentleman rider, for it was well known that he was above suspicion, and had never been guilty of any underhand action. He was young and good-looking, and this was an advantage with the ladies and not disregarded by his own sex. Many bright eyes glanced at him as he stood in a contemplative frame of mind, his top-coat open, showing the blue jacket and a peep of the crimson sleeves of Sir Gordon Sefton. Dudley Massie was scrupulously neat in his attire. He did not consider a gentleman rider ought to neglect his riding costume, nor was he anxious to look as much like a professional jockey as possible. He considered himself a cut above some of the 'regular' riders, and consequently was not over-popular with them. He objected to being hail-fellow-well-met with every man that rode in races, and on the course kept himself to himself as much as possible.

Morgan Sherburn was just the opposite of Massie. He swaggered about the paddock and tried to ape the manners and sayings of other riders. His racing costume did not add to his appearance, but detracted from it. He was careless about his attire, and as he walked across the paddock towards his horse he looked like a low-class jockey. His cap was on the back of his head, and he had a straw in his mouth, which he tried to chew into fragments, his face undergoing sundry contortions during

the process. When he came to his horse
he stood with his legs wide apart, his head
poked forward, and his hands holding his whip
across the front of his body. He was soon
surrounded by a crowd of spongers who pro-
fessed to be his ardent admirers. Their conversation was not edifying, and need not be
related. It referred mostly to the eyes, limbs,
and various other parts of Snowstorm's anatomy,
each portion being preceded by a redhot adjec-
tive. Respectable people steered clear of this
circle, but ' Porty ' was not respectable, and
therefore he accosted Sherburn. As they were
speaking Lady Betty came up with a friend.
Lady Betty would not have missed the Grand
National for anything. She loved steeplechasing and adored gentlemen riders, she declared, and the thought that one or two of
them might get their necks broken added to
her zest for the sport. It could not be denied
that Lady Betty looked well. She knew how
to dress, and tailor-made costumes suited her
figure admirably, and the keen cold winds of
March justified her in selecting warm clothing.
Lady Betty would never have put on a rational
dress or have appeared in bloomers. She had
a very good idea of what men thought about
' rational ' females, and of the remarks they

passed about them, and as she wished to stand
well with the men, she dressed in a more
attractive and fascinating style.

Morgan Sherburn looked at her admiringly
as she came up, and he rudely pushed 'Porty'
aside in order to speak to her.

Lady Betty's husband was accustomed to be
pushed out of the way by her ladyship's friends,
but he resented it all the same, and in no one
more so than 'that cad Sherburn.'

'D—— the little beast !' said his lordship ;
'if he hadn't so much money, and I did not
handle some of it, I'd hope he would break his
neck in the race. Being as it is, I sincerely
trust he will have a very bad fall and smash a
few ribs or something of that kind.'

With which amiable wish he walked away,
taking no notice of Lady Betty.

'You look charming,' said Sherburn. 'You
improve with age, Lady Betty.'

Sherburn liked to say nasty things to Lady
Betty, because he knew she would not resent
them. She ignored his remark, and said

'Am I to back Snowstorm ?'

'Please yourself,' he said. 'I think he will
win.'

'I can get a hundred to twelve about him.'

'Take it,' said Sherburn.

Lady Betty leaned forward and said in a whisper: 'May I back him to win five hundred, and have the wager put down to you—I'm awfully hard up, Morgan?'

'You always are,' he growled. 'You're a perfect leech, Betty.'

'Leeches are useful sometimes,' she said.

'All right; but you may as well make it a thousand, because he has a real good chance.'

'A thousand thanks,' said Lady Betty. 'You are too good, Morgan.'

'Nonsense!' he said roughly; 'I know what I am doing.'

Lady Betty would have liked to strike him in the face had she dared. As this way of showing her gratitude was not permissible, she walked away in order to let her temper cool down.

Sir Gordon Sefton saw Morgan Sherburn talking to Lady Betty, and it did not improve his opinion of his son-in-law. Sir Gordon knew the character Lady Betty bore, and therefore was not surprised to find her on confidential terms with Sherburn.

'I should not be at all surprised if her ladyship has had a hand in spreading this scandal,' he thought. 'She and her husband are a precious pair.'

Dudley Massie was seeing The Slogger put to rights when Sir Gordon came up.

'What do you think of it now?' asked Sir Gordon.

'I think we shall win, but it will be a good race. How is the betting?'

'Donnybrook is favourite at six to one; Snowstorm is well backed at a hundred to twelve; The Slogger I have just accepted fifteen "ponies" about; and I took five hundred to ten about Off Chance. A lot of them are backed, but the Irish money has gone on Donnybrook with a rush. Here's O'Hara. Let us see what he has to say.'

On being questioned, the Irish jockey expressed his conviction that Donnybrook would win.

'It's awful bad luck for me,' said O'Hara. 'Eileen beat him at Punchestown, and it is because she has been struck out they are piling the money on him. Kavanagh will have a nice ride, you bet.'

'I have put you a trifle on Off Chance and The Slogger,' said Sir Gordon.

'Thank you, sir,' said O'Hara; but he wished the money had been on Donnybrook.

Fred Lostock, escorting Lady Sefton and her daughters, joined the group, and Morgan

Sherburn saw them. He did not, however, come to speak to his wife.

Ena Sherburn felt her position keenly, as a proud injured woman would naturally do. She could not fail to notice that she was an object of curiosity to many people, and when she overheard the remark, 'That's Mrs. Sherburn. Good-looking woman, isn't she? They say she's thrown over Sherburn for Dudley Massie. I admire her taste, but it's hardly the thing, you know!' it caused her blood to boil, and made her hate Morgan Sherburn as she had never hated him before. Could a look have killed the speaker he would not have had long to live. The man did not intend she should hear his remark, and slunk away abashed as he caught her eyes.

Dudley Massie was pleased to see the ladies, for he liked them to take an interest in Sir Gordon's horses.

'How well The Slogger looks,' said Ena. 'He does you credit, Mr. Massie.'

'Yes, he looks very well,' said Lady Sefton, who knew nothing at all about horses.

Beatrice remained silent. She did not care to speak with Ena's keen eyes searching her through and through. She felt Ena knew her secret, and it made her feel uncomfortable.

'It will not be long before we find out if he
is as good as he looks,' said Massie. 'I hope
he will win, but Donnybrook must have a great
chance, from the way he is being backed.'

Fred Bexley stood a short distance from the
group, and Dudley saw the horse-dealer wished
to speak to him. When Sir Gordon accompanied the ladies to the stand, he went over to
Bexley, who said :

'I have come across a bit of information
that may be useful to you. Tommy Ranger
rides Crossbar and Ivory First Flight, as you
are aware. Well, both these fellows are in
with Morgan Sherburn. Their horses have
no chance, and I am told Sherburn has paid
them to keep a clear course for him if they can
at the first few jumps. Also, if they see a
chance to interfere with The Slogger, they are
not to let it slip. Never mind how I got to
know, and keep the information to yourself, only
look out for squalls, and steer clear of them.'

'Thanks,' said Massie. 'I know you would
not mention this had you not good grounds for
what you say. I have some idea of what
Ranger and Ivory are capable of, for I have
ridden against them before. Ranger I once
brought a complaint against for foul riding, and
he nearly lost his license.'

'Then you may bet he has not forgotten the incident,' said Bexley. 'Forewarned is forearmed, and you can never know too much about a race before the start.'

Dudley Massie knew that Fred Bexley had a variety of sources of information open to him. He therefore paid more attention to what he had said than under other circumstances he might have done. He knew Sherburn would not stick at trifles, if by doing so he could cause The Slogger to lose the race. He was glad of the timely warning he had received, and resolved to keep his own counsel and make use of the information. There would be more chance of his defeating Sherburn's plans if he acted as though he knew nothing of them.

'Keep as near to me as you can,' he said to O'Hara. 'You will be able to judge what chance you have from the way in which The Slogger is going. Remember, you are to win if you can, but I think I shall beat you.'

O'Hara promised to ride Off Chance as Dudley Massie desired, and the result of the race proved that Jim O'Hara was as good as his word.

CHAPTER XXIII.

THE GRAND NATIONAL.

THE grand stand was crowded before the parade, Lord Derby's box being occupied by an aristocratic party, for his lordship has always been a great supporter of Liverpool races. The stands were thronged with people, and a dense crowd lined up along the iron rails to see the horses go past. The roar of the betting-ring waxed louder and louder as the time drew near for the race. Anxious faces denoted that the result of the race was of great importance to hundreds of people, who would be glad when the suspense was ended. In the paddock many men still lingered, in the hope of obtaining the very latest tip before the horses went out. Here and there could be seen a jockey mounted, and waiting for the order to go out, and others were standing by their mounts in readiness to get into the saddle.

Dudley Massie passed close to Morgan Sherburn, who was already mounted on Snow-storm, and walking the horse about the pad-dock.

'Take care where you are going,' said
Dudley, as Sherburn pulled Snowstorm on to
him.

'You should clear out of the way !' was the
reply. 'If you block me in the race, I shall
soon shift you !'

'You mean you will try,' said Dudley.
'Take my advice, and do not attempt any
of your tricks with me. I have been injured
quite enough by your slander, and I am not in
a temper to let you off easily. If you interfere
with me in the race I shall make it hot for you.'

Sherburn laughed, as he said

'You haven't got the pluck to ride straight;
you prefer an open gate to a stiff fence.'

Dudley Massie made no reply, but Sherburn's words did not improve his temper, and
he meant to be even with him before long.

As the first lot of horses left the paddock to
take part in the parade, Dudley Massie got
into the saddle. The Slogger was the last
to leave the paddock, Snowstorm being in
the first lot. There were twenty-eight runners,
and it was a glorious sight as they paraded in
front of the stand, with the new colours of the
riders flashing in the occasional bursts of sun-
light.

Sundry remarks were passed about the horses

as they went by, for there is often a great difference in a horse when seen in the paddock as compared with his movements on the course. How many men have suddenly changed their opinions after a preliminary gallop, and often to their cost. It is the man who is undecided until the last moment who brings grist to the bookmaker's mill. Many a five-pound note is invested upon a horse because he 'went so well in the preliminary,' and then finished nowhere.

Fred Lostock was one of these men. He backed horses weeks before the race, and then changed his mind at the last moment. It was so on this occasion. Fred stood to win a good stake on The Slogger, but the way the Irish horse Donnybrook moved fascinated him, and he went into the ring to back the Irish candidate. He met Baxter, who asked him what he was going to do.

'I must have a hundred on Donnybrook,' said Fred; 'he goes so well. I shall be savage if he wins, and I have nothing on.'

'I thought you fancied The Slogger,' said Baxter. 'I've backed him, and, take my tip for it, he'll win if there are no accidents. I know The Slogger well. Keep your hundred in your pocket, and stand what you have got.'

'Thanks all the same,' said Fred, 'but I cannot let Donnybrook run loose.'

'How many horses have you backed?' asked Baxter.

'The Slogger, Snowstorm, Freedom, and I want a hundred on the favourite,' said Fred.

'You're a good customer to the bookies. No wonder they win money, when there are men like you about,' said Baxter.

'Pray how many horses have you backed?' asked Fred, nettled at Baxter's remark.

'One, The Slogger. I've backed him for a win and a place, and I'll bet you a fiver he beats Donnybrook, Snowstorm, and Freedom. That's what I think of your little lot,' said Baxter.

'I'll take that,' said Fred, producing a ponderous betting-book.

'How many of those do you fill in a year?' said Baxter, laughing. 'I can write all the wagers I make on my shirtcuff.'

'Dirty habit,' said Fred.

'It has this advantage,' said Baxter 'it all comes out in the washing, and you can start with a clean cuff next time. Besides, bad wagers are better rubbed out, and I can always remember the good ones, they are so few and far between.'

'I like to look over my betting-book at the end of the year,' said Fred.

'No doubt it is interesting reading,' replied Baxter. 'It reminds you of the many good things you have been on that did not come off.'

'If I stand here talking to you I shall not get that hundred on Donnybrook,' said Fred.

'Then remain talking to me by all means,' said Baxter; but Fred Lostock rushed off into the ring.

'Fancy a fellow backing three or four horses in a race,' said Baxter. 'One's enough for me, anyhow.'

The Slogger made a good many friends as Massie rode him past the stands. The horse moved freely, and was well trained and fit to run a severe race—such was the verdict of some of the old hands.

Donnybrook was, however, the great attraction. The Irish horse was a big upstanding bay, nearer seventeen than sixteen hands, and built in proportion to his size. He had powerful quarters and sound front legs which would stand him in good stead over the heavier ground. His back and loins were strong enough to carry almost any weight in reason.

'There can be no doubt the favourite is a splendid horse,' said Sir Gordon to Fred Lostock, who had just regained the stand after a desperate struggle, and was very red in the face and out of breath. 'Where have you been?' asked Sir Gordon, as he noticed Fred's condition. 'You look rather uncomfort able.'

'A bit out of breath, that's all,' said Fred. 'I had a struggle to reach you again. I've put a trifle on the favourite, as I did not like to let him run against me.'

'If I had no horse in the race I should certainly back Donnybrook,' said Sir Gordon.

Lady Betty occupied a conspicuous position on the stand, and, much to his surprise, her husband found himself at her side. It was such a strange thing for them to be together that Porty was tickled at the idea, and laughed to himself in a way he had when amused.

'Don't make that horrid noise,' said Lady Betty. 'I call it a demoniacal chuckle.'

'Can't help it,' said her husband. 'Seems so strange to find myself next to you, Bet.'

'I did not ask you to come. I had much rather you planted yourself elsewhere,' she said. 'I don't appreciate you.'

' No, I'm afraid not,' he said ; ' and yet there's something about me that you ought to appreciate.'

' And pray what is that ?' asked Lady Betty.

' My cursed good-nature !' said Porty, with a leer that made the colour mount into Lady Betty's face, and caused her rouge to take second place.

' There's Snowstorm,' said her ladyship's friend, who saw signs of a domestic breeze that might grow into a storm.

' D—— Snowstorm !' growled Porty; ' I hope his rider will break his '—he was about to say neck—' ribs or his leg.'

' Perhaps you are not aware I stand to win a thousand on Snowstorm,' said Lady Betty.

' Shows your bad taste,' he said ; ' why did you not back my horse ?'

' Because it has no chance. Bexley knows what a fool you are about horses, and he can palm anything off on to you,' she said.

' That's where you make the mistake. I flatter myself I am a judge of horses and women,' he replied.

Lady Betty laughed as she said :

' My dear, you are much too old to talk like

that. I married you because I had compassion upon you. I am an excellent nurse, as you will find out before long.'

'I may be older than you, Bet,' he said; 'but you have made good use of your time, and if there is any wickedness afloat you know how to be in it. That's where you beat me badly.'

'Will you kindly stop talking? I want to see the race, and not have my pleasure spoiled by your continual snarling. I hope Snowstorm will win, and that your pleasant wishes about Morgan Sherburn will not be realized,' said Lady Betty.

'If Sherburn broke a leg it would keep him out of mischief for a time. He couldn't do much harm lying on his back. I'm afraid you would miss him very much.'

'You would miss him more when your money ran short,' was the retort.

'It is awfully hard luck that a little cad like Sherburn has millions, and the representative of an ancient family like myself should positively be hard up,' said Portsdown.

'It is because your family is so ancient that the present representative is in such a decayed state, I suppose,' said Lady Betty.

'If you had lived a few hundred years back

you would have had your tongue cut out for that remark,' said her husband. 'I should like to see some of those ancient punishments revived.'

'It is lucky for you there is no chance of that,' said Lady Betty, 'or you would have lost your head long ago, and your visage would have appeared on a long pole in some conspicuous place.'

'They are at the post now,' said Lady Betty's friend, and Porty fumbled with his glasses in his anxiety to see all there was to be seen.

A breakaway occurred before the flag was hoisted, and two or three horses galloped a considerable distance.

Dudley Massie kept well away from Snow-storm, and found himself between O'Hara on Off Chance and Ranger on Crossbar, who was inclined to be restless and lashed out savagely once or twice.

'Keep away from that brute, or you'll get your horse kicked,' said O'Hara to Dudley, who backed The Slogger out of Crossbar's way.

They were not kept long at the post, for in a few minutes the flag fell, and the lot went away on their long journey

The first to break the line was Oatmeal, but

on settling down First Flight went to the front,
and entered the country clear of Snowstorm,
Off Chance, and one or two more, with The
Slogger about tenth.

Beecher's Brook was reached and cleared
in splendid style, only one horse out of the
twenty-eight runners coming down.

Dudley Massie was in high spirits as he felt
how well The Slogger cleared the famous
jump.

'If he only does it as well at the second
attempt,' thought Dudley, 'there will be a good
chance of winning.'

At the canal fence three horses came to
grief, and one of them continued on his way
riderless.

'I'll keep clear of him,' thought Dudley.
'There's nothing more dangerous than a riderless horse getting in the way.'

As they came on to the racecourse for the
first time, First Flight still led, and was making
the pace hot, and O'Hara on Off Chance was
close after him. The favourite, The Slogger
and Snowstorm, were almost level as they went
past the number board, and all were going
well.

'By Jove!' said Fred Lostock, 'your horse
is galloping as well as the favourite. What

sweeping strides they have! Massie means to keep near Donnybrook. I don't blame him, for the Irish horse has a real good jockey on him. That's an Australian running behind them. Hickey rides a bit different to our fellows, but he's a rare judge of pace, and I've seen him all there in a tight finish.'

There was some cheering as the horses went past, but the finish was too far off for the excitement to be raised to fever height.

Fred Bexley stood close to the rail, and as he saw The Slogger go past with his long, sweeping stride, he said to himself:

' I'm dashed glad I didn't let Sherburn have that horse back. He's not a man I care about. He'll be wild if The Slogger beats Snowstorm. I could have told him it was odds on that before he started. Off Chance goes well. I must try and buy him after the race. Portsdown's old horse is going better than I expected, but he's no chance. That Australian fellow is not much to look at, but he jumps well and moves freely ; a bit short of pace, I should fancy. Hardly so much blood in him as our fellows. That's a fault they will remedy in time. Hallo! that you, Bill ?' he remarked to a big man who put his hand on Bexley's shoulder.

'Yes, I'm all here, Fred,' said William

Branch, a well-known member of the ring.
'What do you fancy?'

'The Slogger,' said Bexley.

'Why? Do you know much about him?'

'Yes; I sold him to Massie for Sir Gordon
Sefton. He's a good horse.'

'Worth having a bit on?'

'Yes; I have backed him,' said Bexley. 'Do
you stand badly against him?'

'He's not my worst. Snowstorm and Donnybrook take most out of the book.'

'The Slogger will beat them,' said Bexley.

'You're a good judge,' said Branch. 'I'll
have a hundred on The Slogger if I can get a
fair price;' and he walked away.

CHAPTER XXIV

AT BEECHER'S BROOK.

THE pace was beginning to tell on the bulk of
the horses, and several of them were tiring
fast. The Australian horse fell back beaten,
and was pulled up.

Dudley Massie took a look round as they
neared the famous brook, and saw close behind
him Crossbar, Off Chance, and Snowstorm,

while in front of him were First Flight and a couple more.

Sherburn eased Snowstorm, but why Massie was unable to make out, as he could see the horse was going well. Donnybrook was on the left, and also galloping in great style. It was an open race at present, and there were more in it at this point than Dudley anticipated.

The nearer they got to the big jump, the more the horses crowded together, and O'Hara thought it would be a lucky chance if they all got over without a spill. None of the riders appeared inclined to give way.

'Go on,' shouted O'Hara to Dudley Massie ; 'they are crowding on to you.'

This was what Dudley expected at some part of the race, but he hardly fancied it would be at Beecher's Brook. He remembered what Fred Bexley said to him, and urged The Slogger on, in order to get a clear jump if possible.

Sherburn again gave Snowstorm his head, and soon raced alongside The Slogger. On the other side, Ranger on Crossbar was going dangerously near to Massie's mount, while Ivory on First Flight blocked the way in front. It was an awkward fix for Dudley

Massie to be in, but there was no getting out of it.

'I must chance it,' he thought. 'We may all scramble over, but if First Flight comes down I'm done for.'

Jim O'Hara, who was behind Dudley Massie, had a better view of what was going on, and he did not like the look of things. He wondered why Ranger and Sherburn did not steer clear of The Slogger; perhaps they would do so when nearer the jump. No alteration, however, took place, and O'Hara came to the conclusion a dead set was being made at Dudley Massie's mount.

'It's a blackguardly thing to do, jostle a man over such a jump,' thought Jim. 'If there is to be a mess, I must look out for squalls. I'll not see Massie suffer any foul play without trying to stop it.'

'Pull out !' shouted O'Hara to Ranger, who was ahead of him; 'you'll have some of us down.'

Ranger either did not hear him or took no notice of his remark, for he continued straight on the course he was going.

The jump loomed ahead, and Dudley Massie was prepared for anything that might happen. Sherburn pulled Snowstorm closer on to The

Slogger, and Crossbar edged in on the other side. Dudley Massie felt it would be well-nigh impossible for The Slogger to get over safely.

'This is your game,' he muttered, with a savage look at Sherburn. 'You may be beaten at it in a way you do not expect.'

The jump was reached, and the decisive moment was at hand. First Flight rose at the obstacle, and blundered badly. Ivory's mount was in front of The Slogger. Dudley Massie rode straight as a die, for it was his only chance; he could not go to the right or left, on account of Snowstorm and Crossbar. The three horses were almost in line, and Ranger pulled his mount on to The Slogger as he went at the jump. Close behind came Jim O'Hara on Off Chance.

For a moment three horses seemed to be flying the jump together, but The Slogger, being wedged in between the other two, had not a fair chance. The horse did his best, but as he topped the fence, Dudley Massie knew there would be a spill ; and a terrible spill it proved to be. Sherburn had a clear course, and got Snowstorm over safely. First Flight fell heavily, and Crossbar cannoning against The Slogger, the pair came down on the top of the fallen horse.

Jim O'Hara, seeing what happened, made a desperate effort to clear them, but although Off Chance jumped splendidly, it was more than the horse could accomplish, and he rolled back on to the struggling trio. How the remaining horses got over without injuring those that were down will ever remain one of those strange chances so frequent in steeplechases.

The first to extricate himself from the unpleasant predicament was Jim O'Hara, who had been shot right out of the saddle. He was quickly on his feet, and, although he felt stunned, had his wits about him. He took in the situation at a glance. The Slogger had struggled clear of the fallen horses, and was starting off in pursuit of the others, when Jim O'Hara caught him by the bridle as he went past, and, after being dragged some yards, succeeded in pulling him up. In the meantime Dudley Massie, crushed and bruised, had scrambled to his feet. His head felt dizzy, and his right arm hung limp, and there was a racking pain in his right side. He stumbled as he walked along, steering mechanically for Jim O'Hara and The Slogger.

Crossbar had broken his back, and Ranger, his jockey, lay groaning under him. First Flight had a broken leg, and Ivory sat stunned

and bruised on the turf, holding his head between his hands.

'Any bones broken?' said Jim O'Hara, as
Dudley Massie came up.

'Give me a leg up,' Dudley answered.
'Make haste! There may be a chance yet.'

Jim glanced ahead, and saw the field had not
gained any great distance. He lifted Dudley
Massie into the saddle, let go The Slogger's
bridle, and the horse galloped in pursuit.

'I'm out of it, any way,' said O'Hara to himself, as he saw Off Chance careering after the
others.

Then he turned his attention to Ranger,
who was still unable to extricate himself
from the fallen horse.

Having roused Ivory to a sense of the
situation, and what was required of him, with
his assistance O'Hara pulled Ranger from
under Crossbar, and the jockey lay groaning
on the grass, more frightened than hurt, having
had a narrow escape of being killed.

Jim O'Hara stood looking at them, and then
burst out :

'D—— me if it wouldn't have served you
right had both of you broken your necks!
You would not have had the chance of en-
dangering any more lives then. You are either

cursed bad riders or scoundrels, and I fancy
the latter term fits you. You nearly killed
Massie, and I had a narrow squeak. Lord
knows how Off Chance jumped you all ; but
he did, and that saved you. I'll leave you
beggars here, and walk back ; I'm sick of the
sight of you.'

'Go to blazes !' said Ivory   'Who are you,
I'd like to know, to start making accusations ?
You'd better mind what you are saying, or it
will be the worse for you.'

'I'll be very careful what I say if it comes
to going before the stewards,' said O'Hara.
'You fellows will not have much chance of
riding again if you get your deserts, nor that
fellow Sherburn either. I saw the little game
the three of you were at, and much good it has
done you. I should not be surprised if The
Slogger wins after all.'

'Where is he ?' asked Ivory.

'Racing after the field as fast as the wind,'
said O'Hara. 'One or two of 'em have only
to make a blunder, and The Slogger will catch
them.'

Ivory laughed as he said :

'There's not much chance of The Slogger
winning this Grand National, anyhow.'

'I'm glad of that,' said Ranger, who had not

before spoken. 'That chap Massie nearly got me sent up.'

'Oh, that's how the land lies, is it?' said Jim O'Hara. 'Well, take care you are not quite sent up this time, instead of nearly.'

While this conversation was being carried on at Beecher's Brook, Dudley Massie on The Slogger was riding what looked like a hopeless chase. His head swam badly, and he could hardly retain his seat; but he set his teeth and determined not to give in until the judge's box was passed. He was in great pain. The whole of his right side was numbed, and almost useless, and his right arm he thought was broken. In front of him he saw the horses racing, with Donnybrook and Snowstorm at their head. The riderless horse he knew was Off Chance. Strange to say, this riderless horse gave him a gleam of hope. If Off Chance raced up amongst the others, it might cause a diversion in The Slogger's favour He kept a sharp look-out ahead, and urged The Slogger on as well as he was able. The horse had not been injured by the fall, and fenced better than ever, the spill having made him more careful, and not shaken his nerves, or put him out of temper.

Away in front rode Morgan Sherburn on

17

Snowstorm, hugely delighted at the success of his dastardly plans. Alongside of him rode Kavanagh on the favourite, but Sherburn saw with exultation that Donnybrook was not going so well, and he knew Snowstorm had the race in hand. He never gave a thought as to what had happened at Beecher's Brook. He knew there had been a terrible spill, and that a serious accident might have occurred; but what cared he when Snowstorm was winning the great race?

Already he fancied he heard the shouts of the excited people, 'Snowstorm wins!' and he imagined how proudly he would ride his horse to weigh in. It would be an additional pleasure to know how he had beaten Sir Gordon Sefton, and Lady Betty would shower her favours upon him for the bet he had given her.

Snowstorm was going strong and well, and Donnybrook was labouring hard.

'You're beaten, my friend,' thought Sherburn. 'I'll show those Irishmen I'm as good a man as any amongst them. They'll not like to be beaten, but they'll have to put up with it.'

Kavanagh saw that Sherburn's mount was going much better than his own, and he began to feel uneasy. He knew, however, that Donnybrook had a great heart, and would struggle on, beaten or not beaten. So he rode his horse carefully, and with excellent judgment, husbanding all the animal's strength, and keeping him for a great run home, if possible.

Finding Donnybrook dropping back, Morgan Sherburn fancied he had an easy task before him, and did not press Snowstorm. This was exactly what Kavanagh had foreseen. Over-confidence was what he wanted to inspire in Morgan Sherburn. If Sherburn became care-less, there was more chance of Donnybrook gaining an advantage.

Snowstorm entered the racecourse well ahead of the favourite, and a struggling field of horses behind them. Snowstorm looked all over a winner, and Fred Bexley began to curse his bad luck.

' It would have been a "cert" for The Slogger, had all gone well. Why the deuce did not Massie keep out of the way of those ruffians ? Eh, by Jove! what's this ?' he ex-claimed, as he caught sight of the blue jacket and crimson sleeves of Sir Gordon Sefton. ' Hang me if it isn't The Slogger, and Massie's got into the saddle again ! Well done, Dudley! —and The Slogger is going well.'

On the stand there was great excitement. Beatrice Sefton was pale as death, and she had nearly fainted when she heard The Slogger

had fallen. Ena Sherburn concealed her feelings, but there was a tumult in her breast
that she could not quell. She felt Morgan
Sherburn had a hand in the disaster, and she
hated him for it. Sir Gordon Sefton took his
bad luck philosophically, and no one was more
surprised than he when Fred Lostock said
excitedly :

' Massie's in the saddle, and after them again !
Hang me if he will not make a race of it !
Look, Sir Gordon ! those are your colours
right enough, although I can hardly believe
my eyes.'

Sir Gordon Sefton put up his glasses, and
saw what Fred Lostock said was correct, and
that The Slogger was still in the race.

' And that riderless horse is Off Chance,' he
said. ' O'Hara must have had a bad fall. There
goes another down ; they're dropping out. The
Slogger might get a place yet.'

Off Chance was galloping along, and jumping the fences cleverly. The riderless horse
followed Snowstorm and the favourite on to the
racecourse.

At the last fence but one Donnybrook came
down, and Morgan Sherburn felt it was a
hundred to one on his mount now. He was
exulting in the victory before it was gained.
In the distance he heard the shouts that pro-

claim the winner, and they were all for him. There was only one more fence, and, safely over that, he could canter in the easiest of winners. Verily, the fates appeared propitious for Morgan Sherburn.

CHAPTER XXV.

THE LAST FENCE.

SIR GORDON SEFTON thought it very hard lines to lose a Grand National by an accident to his horse. He saw Snowstorm going well, and the last fence within easy distance, so he had no option but to count the race as lost. Many members of the ring were looking over the shoulders of their clerks as they balanced the books, and asking: ' How much does Snowstorm take out ?' There was no necessity for race-glasses, the green jacket and red cap stood out so conspicuously. The shouting had abated, and the thousands of people were carelessly watching Snowstorm as he came at the last fence. Very few spectators took any notice of the riderless Off Chance, who was dangerously near the leader.

Fred Bexley's keen eyes saw there might be a chance yet. This is how the astute horse-dealer made out the case to himself :

'Off Chance must have had about enough of it. When a horse is riderless, it takes an awful lot out of him. If Off Chance jumps the last fence alongside Snowstorm, it's about an even money chance he gives Sherburn's mount a nasty knock.'

Just as Morgan Sherburn was preparing, with every confidence, to negotiate the last fence, he saw the riderless horse alongside him. The appearance of Off Chance at this particular moment startled him, and caused him to lose some of his control. No matter how easily a rider may be winning, there is a certain amount of anxiety for the race to end well, especially when it is such an important event as a Grand National. It was so with Sherburn. He knew Snowstorm could hardly lose, and yet he felt anxious. When he saw Off Chance close on to him, it increased his anxiety, and caused him momentary uneasiness.

At the same time that Snowstorm rose at the fence, Off Chance took off. In doing so, the riderless horse, not being under control, jumped sideways, and swerved on to Snowstorm. It was an unlucky mishap for Morgan Sherburn. Snowstorm stumbled as he landed, fell on his knees, and shot Sherburn over his head. Neither rider nor horse chanced to be hurt, and Sherburn had not lost his hold of the reins. When the crowd fully realized what had happened, a perfect bedlam of sound arose. Never had such an exciting episode been witnessed at Aintree before. People rushed to the railings pell-mell to catch a glimpse of what was going on. Bookmakers hurriedly left their clerks to contemplate the balances alone, and craned their necks in frantic endeavours to see what had become of Snowstorm. Hundreds of people on the stands swayed to and fro in their intense excitement, like trees in a gale of wind.

Lady Betty dropped her glasses, and cried out as though she were hurt. She saw a thousand pounds she had considered safe in her pocket slipping out again with uncomfortable rapidity.

Fred Lostock said, ' Well, I'm d——d !' and forgot to be polite in the presence of ladies.

Sir Gordon Sefton exclaimed :

' He's down ! he's down ! Massie has a chance now !'

' Porty ' chuckled gleefully, and muttered :

' I wouldn't have missed this for a thou. !'

Jim O'Hara, who was making his way across the course, stood still and exclaimed :

' Strike me lucky if he ain't down !'

Dudley Massie saw the spill, and a feeling of exultation possessed him. He forgot all about the pain he was in—all he knew was that there remained a chance of winning if he could get The Slogger over the last fence before Sherburn remounted. He thought it could be done, but he would only be just in the nick of time. Kavanagh had remounted Donnybrook, and was coming on behind The Slogger. Several riders who had considered their mounts out of it set them going again, in the hope of gaining a place.

Morgan Sherburn saw The Slogger coming, and ground his teeth together in his rage. That blue jacket with crimson sleeves seemed to blind him with furious disappointment. He roughly jerked Snowstorm's bridle, and the horse backed. The nearer Sherburn tried to get to him, the farther Snowstorm shifted away.

A torrent of imprecations poured from Sherburn's lips, and his rage well-nigh choked him. He had lost control over himself, and was dangerous. At last he got his foot in the stirrup and scrambled into the saddle, as Snowstorm started off, and The Slogger cleared the last fence, with Donnybrook not many lengths behind.

The excitement was now at fever-heat. All three horses had been down and then remounted, and were fighting out the finish for the famous race. Such a thing had never been

known before, but there is no telling what
extraordinary event will happen in a steeplechase. The people cheered until they were
hoarse, and shouted first one horse's name and
then another. Sir Gordon Sefton could not
speak ; the tension was too great, and he wished
the race over.

Ena Sherburn felt a strange delight as she
saw The Slogger racing hard after Snowstorm,
and Beatrice was trembling with nervous fears.
Fred Lostock was cheering at the top of his
voice. He said afterwards if he had not done
so he would have exploded with excitement.
Fred Bexley lost his usual *sang froid* when
witnessing a race, and waved his hat frantically,
at the same time shouting :

'The Slogger wins ! The Slogger wins ! A
" pony " on The Slogger !'

How Dudley Massie rode this great finish
he hardly knew. His descriptive powers failed
him when he tried to give an account of it after
the event.

As they neared the winning-post Morgan
Sherburn thought :

'I shall win ; I shall win.'

Off Chance had already passed the post,
and Sir Gordon said, with a faint smile :

'One of my horses is first past the judge's
box, at any rate.'

By a desperate effort, which caused him excruciating pain, Dudley Massie got The Slogger alongside Snowstorm, and the pair were now racing neck and neck, with Donnybrook some yards in the rear.

Morgan Sherburn's heart failed him at this critical point, and he raised his whip and lashed out in his fury, striking The Slogger over the head, whether by accident or intentionally could hardly be told. But hundreds of people saw the foul blow, and a roar of angry rage broke from them. Morgan Sherburn was as unpopular as Dudley Massie was popular, and the crowd were ready to believe any ill of him. Sherburn had on several occasions 'gone for the public,' and that long-suffering army of small backers knew it.

When the blow fell on The Slogger's head, the horse swerved and faltered in his stride, but Dudley Massie kept him going. They were only a few yards from the judge's box, and The Slogger had his nose in front. Inch by inch the distance gained by Massie's mount increased until it was a clear head that stretched out in front of Snowstorm. Another roar broke forth from the thousands of excited people :

'Slogger wins ! Slogger wins !'

Sherburn heard it, and his face went a ghastly colour. He had been so certain of victory. How confident he felt, and reasonably so, before that last fence was reached! What a change occurred in a few brief moments! Had Sherburn lost thousands of pounds over the race, it would have mattered little to him. A thousand to him did not mean as much as a sovereign to many of those present. It was the thought that all his plans had failed, and that he was being beaten on the post by Massie of all men, his hated rival in sport and in love, that caused him to turn purple with rage and disappointment.

Amidst a scene of unparalleled excitement, Dudley Massie steered The Slogger home, a winner by barely a length from Snowstorm, with Donnybrook in third place, and landed the most sensational of Grand Nationals for Sir Gordon Sefton.

As the tired horses returned to weigh in the crowd became very excited. Dudley Massie was cheered again and again, and it was noticed how deadly pale he became, and his face twitched as though he were in great pain. Morgan Sherburn was received with some cheers, but they were drowned amidst the hootings and groanings that accompanied them. Kavanagh, on Donnybrook, came in for a burst of applause. Sir Gordon Sefton, with Fred Lostock, hastened down to his horse.

Dudley Massie dismounted with difficulty, took off the saddle, and staggered into the weighing-room.

'All right!' was quickly pronounced, and again the cheering was renewed.

The Slogger was led away, followed by an admiring crowd.

Jim O'Hara made his way up to Dudley Massie, and said

'I'm right glad you won. It serves those scoundrels right. Are you going to bring them before the stewards?'

Dudley Massie thanked O'Hara with a faint smile. He was leaning heavily on Sir Gordon and Fred Lostock, and looked feeble and shattered.

'He's badly hurt,' said Fred Lostock. 'I'm going to take him to the Adelphi at once. You'd better help me, Jim. Sir Gordon must return to the ladies.'

'Can you stand it until you reach the hotel?' said O'Hara. 'You will be more comfortable there.'

'Yes,' said Massie faintly.

Sir Gordon saw them safely into a cab, and then returned to the stand. He explained what had happened, and Beatrice, who could control her feelings no longer, said

'Is he badly hurt? Is there any danger?

Will he want a nurse ?   Let me go and nurse him, father !'

'Beatrice,' said her mother severely, 'please do not make an exhibition of yourself here.'

'I don't care,' said the usually mild Beatrice to her surprised mother. 'If he's in danger, I will attend to him. It is through us he has been injured.'

'You are talking nonsense,' said Ena. 'Mr. Massie will be well looked after.'

'Perhaps you wish to nurse him yourself ?' said Beatrice, in a low voice.

'How dare you speak to me like that !' said Ena. 'There is no necessity for nursing. If he were dying I could not nurse him, and you know it.'

Beatrice had a lovable disposition, and the way Ena spoke the last sentence startled her.

'I am sorry I said that, Ena. Please forgive me.'

Ena Sherburn did not answer, and her sister looked at her pityingly.

'It must be terrible to love when it is hopeless,' thought Beatrice. 'And she is Morgan Sherburn's wife ;' and the young girl shuddered.

Ena was indeed paying dearly for her mistake in marrying Sherburn. She had no one to blame but herself, and this did not make her burden any easier to bear.

A rumour quickly spreads on a racecourse, and it was soon freely talked about that there had been some foul riding.

The stewards heard of it, but as no complaint had been made, they doubted it. Still, they had seen Morgan Sherburn strike The Slogger over the head, and knowing that rider's character, it made them think there might have been something wrong. They knew Dudley Massie had been removed from the course to his hotel seriously injured, and that he could make no complaint.

Jim O'Hara did not mean to let Ranger and Ivory off so easily, and he made a complaint to the stewards. After hearing what O'Hara had to say, they decided to adjourn the matter until Dudley Massie could give his version of the affair at Beecher's Brook.

Morgan Sherburn cursed his luck, and called O'Hara a meddling fool, who had no right to interfere in the matter. He saw Lady Betty after the race, and vented his ill-humour upon her in such an insulting manner that she resolved to make him pay dearly for it.

'If I could only get rid of him,' she thought, 'I should be a better woman. Should I enjoy being a good woman? I doubt it.'

CHAPTER XXVI.

AT THE ADELPHI HOTEL.

THE injuries Dudley Massie received in the Grand National were more serious than at first anticipated. He had suffered some internal injury that the doctors decided would retard his recovery considerably. He could not be removed from the Adelphi Hotel, and Fred Lostock decided to remain with him.

Sir Gordon and Lady Sefton, accompanied by their daughters, returned home, and Beatrice found it a constant strain upon her to answer the continual questions her brother asked her about his favourite, Dudley Massie. She was very much in love with Dudley, but did not wish him to have any idea such was the case, although she thought Arthur pleaded her cause in that direction. She did not wish him to do so, but she was helpless in the matter, because when Arthur made up his mind to do a thing he managed to attain his object somehow.

Although Dudley Massie was not in great pain, and had no bones broken, his shoulder having been put out, he had to remain perfectly quiet. The slightest cause for irritation made his head ache and swim in the most painful manner.

'It is an awful bore lying here day after day,' he said to Fred Lostock. 'Try and persuade these doctors to let me go home, for I am certain I shall never get well until they do.'

'You're mending fast,' said Fred. 'Have a little patience, old man, and you'll soon pull round.'

'It is all very well for you to talk like that,' said Dudley 'You can go out and walk about, and enjoy yourself thoroughly.'

Fred Lostock did not allow Dudley Massie to talk long in this strain. He generally managed to change the conversation successfully.

'Have you made up your mind what to do about O'Hara's complaint to the stewards?' asked Fred.

'I wish he had let the whole affair slide,' said Dudley. 'No good can come of it. Jim O'Hara cannot prove anything, and I shall not say much if I am compelled to give evidence.'

'But you ought to do so,' said Fred. 'Such a scoundrel as Sherburn ought to be shown up, and severely dealt with.'

'How can you deal severely with a millionaire?' asked Dudley.

'Hang his money!' said Fred. 'You'll see with the stewards that will not stand him in good stead.'

'Sherburn's money pays for a multitude of sins,' said Dudley.

'It pays for a lot of Lady Betty's sins, no doubt,' said Fred. 'By the way, I heard he had fallen out with her ladyship. Said some very nasty things to her after the National, and she is not the kind of woman to stand that, even from him.'

'I believe Lady Betty circulated the scandal about Mrs. Sherburn,' said Dudley.

'Very likely,' said Fred; 'but don't you bother your head about that, for no one believes it.'

When Dudley Massie had been at the Adelphi a fortnight, Fred Lostock bounced into his room one morning, evidently bursting with news of importance.

'What's up now?' asked Dudley. 'Is the Derby favourite dead lame, or have you come into a fortune? Out with it quick. I see it will not keep.'

'It was by the merest chance I heard the news in confidence,' said Fred. 'I met a legal friend in Church Street, and we had a long chat together. What do you think he told me?'

'I'm not good at conundrums of any kind,' said Dudley, 'and anything connected with the

18

legal profession must be very difficult to solve. I hope you are in no serious trouble. Is it breach of promise ?'

' No, it's divorce,' said Fred.

Dudley Massie held up his hands with a gesture of horror.

' I should never have thought it of you, Fred. Who is the lady ?'

' Don't be a fool ! You are lying there partially helpless, and know you are safe, or I would chastise you for your insolence. I am not likely to be such a consummate ass as to mix myself up in such a nasty business as divorce !' said Fred.

' Then, what is the interesting news ? If it does not concern yourself, it must be an ordinary affair.'

' But that's just what it is not,' said Fred. ' I think there is something fishy about the whole thing, but my legal friend says not.'

' Out with it !' said Dudley, who was interested in spite of himself.

' Well, Porty's bringing an action for divorce against Lady Betty, and Morgan Sherburn is the co-respondent,' said Fred, pausing to watch the effect of his announcement.

Dudley Massie was astonished. He would not have been surprised to hear that Ena Sherburn had decided to try for a separation from her husband, but he never thought Portsdown would bring an action against Lady Betty. He saw at once that if Portsdown won his case, and Morgan Sherburn was mulcted in heavy damages, Ena Sherburn would have no difficulty in winning her case if she took proceedings. That, he fancied, would alter the course of her life somewhat.

'You have surprised me,' he said to Fred, 'and I hope you are satisfied. I should never have given Porty credit for any move so daring.'

'I thought it was a put up job, and said as much,' said Fred.

'And your legal friend snubbed you?' asked Dudley.

'He did let me down a shade,' said Fred. 'But even now, with his assurance, I can hardly believe it.'

'How will such an action go?' asked Dudley.

'There will be no difficulty in proving the facts, I imagine,' said Fred. 'The question is whether Porty will come out of it with clean hands.'

'I cannot see Portsdown's object,' said Dudley. 'Had he wished to divorce Lady Betty, he could have done so long ago; she has given him ample opportunity.'

'I think he fancies he will be awarded heavy

damages against Sherburn, and he hates him like poison,' said Fred.

'It generally comes to pass,' said Dudley, 'that when a man has been under monetary obligations to another man he hates and despises him. Perhaps you are right in your idea, but Porty will have to be very careful if he is to succeed. There are some very black marks against his name.'

Sir Gordon Sefton was determined when Massie had recovered that Ena should bring an action against Morgan Sherburn for a separation. He thought sufficient evidence might be forthcoming to warrant such an action being taken. It was therefore with considerable surprise he heard the news at his club of the action to be brought by Portsdown against Lady Betty. This would be an excellent way of settling Morgan Sherburn, and he heartily hoped the action would be successful.

Sir Gordon did not at all like the idea of his daughter proceeding against Morgan Sherburn so soon after her marriage, but as he had no doubt his son-in-law caused the fictitious telegram to be sent from Paris, and had circulated a number of abominable slanders, he felt it was only just that Sherburn should be brought to book.

About a week after he heard of this rumour, Sir Gordon met Morgan Sherburn at the Fistic Club, and, much to his son-in-law's surprise, the baronet spoke to him.

'Wants to pump me about the Lady Betty affair,' thought Sherburn. 'He's welcome to all he can get out of me.'

'By the way,' said Sir Gordon, after a few moments' conversation, 'is this true about Portsdown bringing an action against his wife, and that you are implicated?'

Sherburn laughed harshly, and said :

'The old idiot may bring his action, for all I care! I have heard nothing official about it. If Lady Betty brought an action against Porty for refusing to maintain his wife, she would probably be successful.'

'That may be as you say,' said Sir Gordon, nettled at the flippant manner in which Sherburn spoke ; 'but it is totally beside the more important question of an action for divorce in which you are named as a co-respondent. I have to consider my daughter in this matter.'

'You ought to have considered a couple of months ago, before we were married !' retorted Sherburn.

'Quite so,' replied Sir Gordon. 'I am sorry I did not, but one is always liable to make mistakes ; for instance, two months ago I thought you a gentleman, and a man of honour. Now——'

Sir Gordon shrugged his shoulders, and made no comment.

'It matters very little to me whether you consider me a gentleman or otherwise,' said Sherburn. 'I am your daughter's husband, and I mean to have my rights. If you make a move in this matter, so shall I. If an action is brought against me by your daughter, she will have to answer my accusations, in which your gentleman jockey is implicated.'

Had this conversation occurred outside the club, Sir Gordon Sefton would have thrashed Morgan Sherburn for his insolence. He could have accomplished the task with ease and satisfaction. It might have been considered appropriate to knock a man down in a club bearing the name of Fistic; but Sir Gordon knew what clubdom demanded of him, and refrained from gratifying a momentary inclination. It had been Sir Gordon's intention to take no action over the complaint made by Jim O'Hara after the Grand National, but he changed his mind when Morgan Sherburn had spoken, and said :

'I think it only fair to warn you I shall support O'Hara in his complaint about foul riding in the National. I shall also request Massie to tell everything to the stewards, and expose anything there may be to expose. I have heard he received a warning before the race that there would be a dead set made at my horse, The Slogger, and that you were the instigator of the dastardly business. I hope you will not only get your deserts in the divorce court, or any other court, but that the stewards will have sufficient evidence placed before them to warrant them in warning you off.'

'An excellent speech,' said Morgan Sherburn. 'I am proud to have such a father-in-law. You are a credit to me, and again I say, I am proud of you. Having won the Grand National by a mere fluke, you now wish to cast aspersions upon me. You will not succeed by fair means ; but if you happen to be successful, I will make you repent your action to your dying day.'

'Indeed,' said Sir Gordon, 'I shall never repent having exposed you.'

'Wait and see,' said Sherburn. 'You are proud of the name you bear, but it shall be dragged in the mud through your daughter, my charming wife. I was fooled into settling money upon her——'

'Stop!' said Sir Gordon ; 'you need not

allude to that.   My daughter would refuse to touch your money now.'

'We shall see,' said Sherburn.   'At present, take care how you act.'

Sir Gordon Sefton was in a vindictive mood after his meeting with Morgan Sherburn. Before he had cooled down he found himself seated in a first-class carriage, and being rapidly whirled on his way to Liverpool.   He had not seen Massie more than once since the accident, knowing he was well looked after by Fred Lostock.

'He didn't seem inclined to move in the matter, or to back O'Hara up when I saw him,' thought Sir Gordon.   'I can talk him over, I think.   I wonder if he ever was in love with Ena?   Now, if he'd fallen in love with Beatrice I should not have been surprised. Ena would never give him the slightest encouragement, she's too proud.   Her pride did not do her much good when she selected Sherburn as a partner for life, or for some portion of her life.   I think Beatrice does love Massie.   If she is inclined that way, she shall have him, if he's willing.   I'll not put obstacles in her way, for Dudley Massie is a downright good fellow.   This cad Sherburn must be settled with, somehow.   There'll be a lot of scandal, and the public will gloat over it ; but the situation cannot be worse than at present. I wonder what my wife will think of it all ? We have kept her fairly in the dark up to now ; but she will have to know, and the sooner the better. Ena is the one to tell her.'

He gave a sigh of relief as he shelved this burden on to Ena's shoulders. Sir Gordon had a dread of explanations with his wife.

When he arrived at Liverpool he walked into the hotel and went to Dudley Massie's rooms.

Needless to say, both Massie and Fred Lostock were surprised to see him, and wondered what had brought Sir Gordon to Liverpool.

Sir Gordon did not leave them long in doubt. He was fresh from his interview with Morgan Sherburn, and he plunged into the matter he had in hand at once.

CHAPTER XXVII.

THE STEWARDS HOLD AN INQUIRY.

WHEN Sir Gordon had fully explained all that took place between himself and Morgan Sherburn at the Fistic Club, Dudley Massie no longer hesitated as to how he should act in the matter of giving evidence before the stewards.

He explained to Sir Gordon Sefton that he had been warned by Fred Bexley, before the race, to steer clear of Ranger and Ivory.

'Then Bexley ought to give evidence,' said Sir Gordon.

'He would not care about doing so,' said Dudley.

'If his name is mentioned, as it must be by you,' replied Sir Gordon, 'he is sure to be called, and then he will be compelled to attend.'

It was intimated to the stewards that Dudley Massie was well enough to appear at the inquiry, and it was held accordingly. All the parties interested were in attendance, and there was some excitement in sporting circles as to the result. Morgan Sherburn had often been guilty of doing shady things in races; but, so far, he had been clever enough to escape being caught. The stewards were not at all disposed to let him off lightly, if there was clear evidence against him.

The inquiry lasted some time, as several witnesses were called. Jim O'Hara gave a clear and accurate account of what took place at Beecher's Brook.

'I was in a position to see everything,' said

Jim, 'as my mount had been behind the leaders for some distance.   I saw Ranger bore into The Slogger, and Mr. Sherburn, on the opposite side, also bored in.   Ivory, on First Flight, blocked the way in front.   It was a barefaced case of shutting The Slogger in, so that he had no chance of clearing the jump.'

'We are the judges of that,' said the chairman.   'We do not want your opinion at present; please confine yourself to what you saw.'

'I saw Crossbar and Snowstorm pulled on to The Slogger,' said O'Hara. 'Had Mr. Massie obtained a clear run, the horse would have got over the jump.   I was close behind, and called to Ranger to pull out.   I do not know whether he heard me; at any rate, he took no notice. When I saw the horses fall, I had to do the best I could for myself.   I set Off Chance at the jump in the hope he would clear the lot, for I had no time to pull up at the pace we were going.'

Jim O'Hara then described how the spill occurred, and what happened afterwards.   He also mentioned what Ranger and Ivory said after the fall.

Dudley Massie's evidence corroborated O'Hara's, but he had more to add to it. He gave an account of his conversation with

Fred Bexley before the race, and of the warning he received. This evidence caused quite a sensation, and Fred Bexley was called to state what he knew.

The horse-dealer said it was perfectly true that he warned Mr. Massie, because he had good reasons for so doing, and the result of the race proved he was right.

Pressed by the chairman, Fred Bexley said his informant stated that both Ranger and Ivory were in Sherburn's pay. He declined, however, to give the name of his informant, which somewhat discounted his evidence, although the stewards believed it to be correct.

'You sold The Slogger to Mr. Massie for Sir Gordon Sefton?' asked the chairman.

'I did,' said Fred, 'and he was a cheap horse. Fancy parting with a National winner in that easy fashion! I'll tell you what it is, gentlemen——'

Bexley was beginning to be loquacious, but the chairman, smiling, said

'I have no doubt you can tell us a good deal, Bexley, but please confine yourself to the matter in hand.'

'Very well,' said Bexley. 'What is it you wish to know?'

'What sort of a horse is The Slogger?' asked the chairman. 'Has he a nasty temper?'

'He has a will of his own, but I should not call him nasty-tempered,' said Bexley.

' Is he a safe jumper ?'

' Yes,' said Bexley emphatically, ' that he is, or you may bet I would not have backed him for the Grand National.'

' You also sold Snowstorm to Mr. Sherburn ?'

' I did, and he's another good horse.'

' Equal to The Slogger ?'

' Oh no ! I bought The Slogger from Mr. Sherburn. I fancy he was sorry he sold him when he saw how well the horse went in Mr. Massie's hands.'

Several jockeys who rode in the race were called, but could not throw much light upon the subject. Ranger and Ivory denied everything, and the former spoke bitterly about Dudley Massie having complained of him before.

Upon being cross-questioned, Ranger admitted he had on several occasions received presents from Mr. Sherburn. He received a sum of money from him the week before the Grand National, but it had nothing whatever to do with that race. Ivory also acknowledged he had received money from Mr. Sherburn at various times.

Morgan Sherburn gave his evidence in a sullen manner. He saw the inquiry was going against him, and it did not improve his temper.

' There was no attempt on my part,' he said, ' to interfere with Mr. Massie's mount. Even had I wished to do so, I should have been a fool for following my inclinations, because Snowstorm would have been quite as likely to come down as The Slogger. Mr. Massie did not ride a good race. When we reached the Brook, he jammed The Slogger between Snowstorm and Crossbar. It was entirely his own fault he got into such a tight place. He wanted the centre of the jump, and that made him reckless, and he dashed in between Ranger and myself. I did not see what took place, as my horse got clear over. Had I jostled The Slogger, I should probably have brought my own mount down. As to giving Ranger and Ivory money, I acknowledge it. I give a good lot of money away at times to fellows who are in want of ready cash, and that is no man's business except my own. As to what Bexley has stated, it is pure nonsense. I know Bexley and his methods well, and having backed The Slogger, he no doubt invented the story he told Mr. Massie, in order to try and persuade him to be very careful. Ranger and Ivory have denied that there is any truth in Bexley's statement, and I believe it was a pure invention.'

When the evidence was concluded, the

stewards consulted for some time. It was somewhat difficult for them to decide. They had no doubt in their own minds that Morgan Sherburn had paid Ranger and Ivory to act as they had done, but the evidence did not prove this. There might be a suspicion that all had not been fair and square on Sherburn's part, but that was not sufficient to warrant them in punishing him.

Eventually the stewards decided to suspend Ranger and Ivory, and they advised Morgan Sherburn to be more careful in future in dealing with jockeys, and giving them money so short a time before a big race.

'That in itself is a suspicious circumstance,' said the chairman; 'but we think it better to give you the benefit of the doubt.'

'I do not want to benefit by any doubt there may be in your minds,' said Sherburn angrily. 'I am perfectly innocent of everything in connection with this miserable business. My name has been brought forward out of pure spite on the part of Sir Gordon Sefton!'

'You are behaving in a very foolish manner,' said the chairman. 'Sir Gordon Sefton did not lay any information against yourself or the other riders. James O'Hara is the complainant. I thought you were aware of that.'

'O'Hara is merely put forward by others

who wish to shield themselves behind his name. I should never have been brought into the affair had it not been for a disagreement I had with Sir Gordon Sefton, who threatened what he would do.'

'Perhaps Sir Gordon Sefton will explain?' said the chairman.

'Certainly,' said Sir Gordon. 'I had an interview with Mr. Sherburn at the Fistic Club. Before that interview I had decided not to come forward in support of O'Hara's complaint, unless called upon by the stewards; after the interview named I changed my mind. That is exactly how the matter stands. It does not make the facts better or worse.'

'Quite right, Sir Gordon : it does not,' said the chairman. 'Have you anything more you wish to say?' he added, turning to Morgan Sherburn.

'It is not much use saying anything here. I can see the stewards are biased against me. They are welcome to all the satisfaction they may get out of it, and I have no doubt I shall survive the ordeal.'

The stewards consulted together for a few minutes, and then the chairman said :

'We have decided not to take any further notice of your remarks, Mr. Sherburn, and, as I said before, we give you the benefit of the doubt. As a much older racing man than yourself, I advise you never to allow your name to be mixed up in such an affair again.'

Morgan Sherburn, after the inquiry, was in a state of boiling indignation against the stewards, Sir Gordon Sefton, Dudley Massie, and everyone connected with the case. He knew the result of the inquiry would appear in the papers, and he hated the thought of people gloating over the censure he had received.

He went home to Park Lane, and determined to drown his bitter feelings in riotous living. He had not been in the house long when Lady Betty called. At first he declined to see her, but she sent back a reply that she should not quit the house until he had seen her.

'Show her up here,' he said to Daly.

'Into this room?' asked the valet.

'Yes, in here,' said Sherburn. 'What's good enough for me is good enough for her!'

It certainly was not a pleasant room for a lady to enter. It reeked of stale tobacco-smoke and the fumes of brandy that had been spilt on the carpet. Ends of cigars were on the table, and it was evident the place had not been cleaned up from the previous night, the reason for this seeming neglect being that Sherburn generally locked it up when he went out, and put the key in his pocket.

Lady Betty entered the room, bringing with her an odour of costly perfume. She glanced round disdainfully, and expressed her disgust by putting a delicate lace handkerchief to her face.

'How the place smells!' she said. 'What do you mean by allowing me to come in here? This is not the place to receive a lady.'

'Never said it was!' growled Sherburn. 'What are you here for, any way?'

'You know why I am here,' she said.

'If you have come about the divorce case, you may as well spare your breath. I have had quite enough worry about it already.'

'You must stop the proceedings,' she said.

He laughed mockingly, and said

'Surely you are not afraid of facing the court, knowing how complete will be the establishment of your innocence?'

'I dare not face the court, and *you* know it. You must see Porty, and buy him off.'

'Not a farthing!' he said. 'Between the pair of you, I have been well drained already.'

'Heavy damages will be awarded against you,' she said, 'and a paltry ten thousand would square matters.'

'Are you quite sure he would take that?' said Sherburn.

'Yes, because proceedings have not been

commenced yet,' she said. 'Do try, for my sake, Morgan ; I could not bear the disgrace.'

''Pon my word, that's good !' he said. 'Why, you ought to have been divorced long ago.'

'Bah !' she said. 'You men never understand. I want to retain the share of respectability that falls to my lot through having a lawful husband. Only think what people would dare to say about me if I became a divorced woman !'

'Some of 'em would be very nasty,' said Sherburn, 'especially those dear people you have crushed so beautifully.'

'Will you see my husband and arrange with him ?' she asked.

'Don't half like the business,' he said. 'You ask him.'

'He will not speak to me,' she said ; 'he lives entirely at his club. Call and see him there. He'll see you, because he will scent money in the air.'

'And if I succeed ?' said Sherburn.

'I shall always be grateful,' she said.

'I'd like to see you grateful,' he replied ; 'it would be a change. I think I'll try it on with Porty.'

'Thanks so much,' she said. 'It will be better for all parties if the thing can be kept out of court. Fancy how the papers would

revel in it, and how all our best friends would
devour the reports instead of their breakfasts!
Think how delightful it will be to balk them
of their morning meal of scandalous details,
served up well seasoned!'

'By Jove! it is worth trying, if only to dis-
appoint people,' said Sherburn. 'I'll lose no
time about it, and let you know the result as
soon as possible.'

CHAPTER XXVIII.

A DISGRACEFUL BARGAIN.

WHEN he came to think over what Lady Betty
had said, Morgan Sherburn rather enjoyed the
idea of 'tackling Porty,' as he termed it.   He
meant to say nasty things to his lordship, and
pay him out for sundry snubbings received.
He cared very little whether he succeeded or
otherwise in his mission.   Proceedings in the
Divorce Court had no terrors for him, and for
Lady Betty's feelings he cared not a jot.

He called at Portsdown's club, and found
Lady Betty's husband alone in one corner of a
large room, seated in an easy-chair, reading a
newspaper.   Hearing someone coming towards
him, Lord Portsdown glanced up and saw
Morgan Sherburn's figure reflected in the glass.

'Wonder what the deuce he wants !' thought Portsdown. 'If he means trying to settle this divorce business with me, he'll find it a tougher job than he expects.'

Morgan Sherburn came forward without the slightest hesitation, and said :

'Glad to see you looking so well. You are quite a juvenile, and never seem to grow older.'

'Can't say the same about you,' replied Portsdown ; 'you look seedy.'

'Perhaps I do; I have had a good deal to bother me lately,' said Sherburn. 'Between Sefton and yourself I have had a deuced lively time. I'm full of it, and that's why I am here.'

'How can I help you ?' said Portsdown. 'I ought to look far worse than you. Think of all I have gone through, mainly owing to your conduct, and what a struggle it has been for me to make up my mind to bring this action.'

'It always was a struggle for you to make up your mind,' said Sherburn. 'There's not much of that commodity about you, and it requires a deal of care to collect the atoms together.'

'If you came here to insult me, let me tell you, once for all, I will not have it !' said Ports- down. 'You are not a member of this club, thank Heaven ! and I can have you turned out.'

'Proceed at once,' said Sherburn. 'You will be the loser by such an action.'

Portsdown made no reply, but took up his newspaper again.

'Put that paper down, and listen to me,' said Sherburn.   'I have an important offer to make you.'

'What sort of an offer?'

'I want you to refrain from taking proceedings against your wife in the Divorce Court,' said Sherburn.

'Then you may take it for granted I shall do nothing of the sort,' said Portsdown.

'You have no chance of winning,' replied Sherburn.   'Apart from the injustice of your accusations, your own moral character will be torn to shreds in such a case.   You haven't a leg to stand on.   If your wife has not been all she ought to be, whose fault is it?   Ask yourself that question.'

'Has my wife requested you to see me?' asked Portsdown.

'She has.   You have declined to communicate with her, and she asked me to see you. Lady Betty is not the guilty woman you imagine her to be.   She may be fast, and misconstruction may be put upon her actions, but she's not half as bad as people make out.   Compared with yourself, the balance is very much in her favour.'

'All this comes well from you,' said Portsdown. 'You appear to know more about her actions than I do.'

'Why do you want a divorce?' asked Sherburn.

'To make you pay for your infamous conduct, and to disgrace my wife,' said Portsdown, turning sharply round and facing him.

Morgan Sherburn laughed, as he replied:

'When I have told my tale in court, you may possibly get a divorce, but that is doubtful. You will certainly not obtain damages. No jury will reward you, after hearing the sort of character I shall give you.'

This reply made an impression upon Portsdown. He knew Morgan Sherburn could produce proofs of certain transactions that would not redound to his credit.

Sherburn gave him time for a few moments' reflection, and then said

'The damages you anticipate are, I presume, to compensate you for the loss of your wife. Would it not be far better to receive the damages without losing Lady Betty? Just think it over.'

'What is the little scheme you hinted at?' asked Portsdown, glancing round to see if anyone was within earshot. They were alone, and he felt relieved.

'Will you stop further proceedings against

your wife, if I agree to compensate you for any injury you imagine you have sustained?' asked Sherburn.

'The injuries are not imaginary,' said Portsdown; 'I wish they were.'

'Oh, stop your croaking!' said Sherburn; 'Lady Betty is quite as good a wife as other women in her set, and a far better one than you deserve. If old men will insist upon marrying handsome young women, they must be prepared to take the consequences.'

'Nothing can compensate a man for loss of honour and self-respect,' said Portsdown loftily.

The idea of Porty talking about honour and self-respect in connection with himself amused Morgan Sherburn, and he burst out laughing.

'Honour and self-respect!' he repeated. 'Granted the loss of such things is severe, you never possessed them, so I fail to see how you can lose them.'

'There is my name to be considered,' said Portsdown. 'I have to uphold the ancient name I bear. It is incumbent upon me to do so. I am the head of a great race.'

'Are you joking, or do you really believe all the rot you are talking?' said Sherburn.

'Make your proposal, and I will see whether I can honourably accept it,' said Portsdown.

'How much will you take not to proceed against your wife?' asked Sherburn—'that's what I mean, in plain language. Do you understand it?'

'You have such a brutal way of putting things,' said Portsdown. 'If I agreed to consider any such offer from you, it would be to spare my name from public disgrace and scandal.'

'Put it that way, if you like,' said Sherburn, ' if it will ease any small fragments of conscience you possess.'

'How much do you propose to offer me to stay proceedings?'

'Five thousand pounds,' said Sherburn.

Portsdown waved his hand, and said :

'You are joking; such a sum is too paltry for me to consider for a moment. Double it, and I will think the matter over.'

'I will double it,' said Sherburn, 'on one condition.'

'And that is?'

'That you take steps to contradict all the paragraphs that have already appeared in print. Write to the papers denying these rumours, and sign your name,' said Sherburn.

'And you agree to give me ten thousand pounds?' said Portsdown. 'When shall I have the money?'

'The day the contradictions appear, signed by you.'

Portsdown smiled as he replied

'And what security have I that you will keep your part of the bargain ?'

'I give you my word I will pay you,' said Sherburn.

'Security not good enough,' said Portsdown.

'Then you can go to the devil, and take what proceedings you please !' said Sherburn. 'You will get no further security from me ;' and he got up and walked towards the door.

'I shall have to trust him,' thought Portsdown. 'He is not likely to go back on his bargain—he will not do that.'

'Come back,' said Portsdown ; 'you need not be in such a hurry.'

Morgan Sherburn returned, and remained standing. Portsdown said :

'I accept your assurance that you will pay me ten thousand pounds, and I will have the letters inserted at once. If you do not fulfil your part of the bargain, it will be an easy matter to say, " Further evidence has been discovered, and the great Portsdown divorce case will come off after all." '

'Then it's settled,' said Sherburn, 'and I'm sorry for you, Portsdown. I had no idea you were such a blackguard. Don't fly into a passion ; you know it is true, and that you have made a disgraceful bargain.'

' I can repudiate it.'

' But you will not do so. I know your selfish, sordid nature too well,' said Sherburn. ' For ten thousand pounds you would sell your soul ; but I expect it is heavily mortgaged already. I can trust you to say nothing of this transaction. Even you dare not mention it.'

When Morgan Sherburn left the room, Portsdown ordered a bottle of wine. He did not relish the thrusts he had received, and required something to wash them down.

He had never felt so utterly mean and small in his life. He knew he had done a disgraceful thing, but he felt some satisfaction that the bargain would never be known.

When Lady Betty heard the news she was jubilant. She could have her revenge now, and the scandalous rumours about her would be contradicted by Portsdown.

No wonder she despised her husband. He believed her guilty of the worst conduct, and she knew other women were far deeper in the mire than herself. This threatened action for divorce had done Lady Betty good, for it had frightened her into a better frame of mind. She began to feel sorry for circulating slanders about Ena Sherburn, and vowed she would do so no more.

As for Morgan Sherburn, after he left Ports-down at the club, he spent a riotous night in town. He visited some well-known haunts, and picked up several of his most undesirable acquaintances. It was after midnight when he reached Park Lane, accompanied by a couple of men of shady reputation.

Raymond Daly heard them come staggering up the stairs, and knew they were more or less intoxicated. He went to bed, and left them drinking. In the morning, when he came down, he found the two men gone, and Morgan Sherburn lying on the hearthrug.

The window was wide open, and the room felt damp and cold. Raymond Daly shut the window, and then tried to rouse his master.

Morgan Sherburn was not a particularly strong man, and constant dissipation, combined with the wasting for riding, had undermined his constitution. With assistance, the valet got him to his bedroom, where he was undressed and put to bed. Next morning he was in a high fever, and the doctor was sent for.

For a few days Morgan Sherburn raved and tossed about in delirium. Raymond Daly attended to him ; but he was not attached to his master, and thought Sherburn's illness a bore. So the young millionaire lay neglected, and there was no kindly hand to soothe his aching head, or smooth his crumpled pillow. The servants heeded him not, but enjoyed themselves to their hearts' content. The doctor remonstrated, but to no purpose, and at last took it upon himself to send in a professional nurse. Raymond Daly made it as uncomfortable for her as possible, and she had the greatest difficulty in getting what she required for her patient.

'You ought to send for his wife,' she said to Daly.

'She would not come near him,' he replied.

'Has he no friends?' asked the nurse.

'He has heaps of people who call themselves his friends,' said Daly; 'but you'd not get one of them to come and see him now.'

'How very sad!' replied the nurse.

'It's his own fault,' said Daly; 'you need not pity him. When he's well again, he'll as like as not round on you.'

'I shall do my duty by him,' said the nurse. 'Are you aware he is dangerously ill?'

'Oh, he'll pull round,' said Daly carelessly and left the room.

The nurse, however, had her doubts as to whether Morgan Sherburn would 'pull round.'

CHAPTER XXIX.

THE HAND OF FATE.

MORGAN SHERBURN groaned and tossed upon his sick-bed for a week, and no one came to inquire how it was he had not appeared about town. Lady Betty did not call to thank him for what he had done, and she had no idea he was ill. Ena Sherburn received a communication from the doctor, but she could not make up her mind to go to her husband. She wrote to the nurse asking for full particulars, which, when received, caused her considerable agitation. Neglected and alone, save for the professional nurse who attended him, Morgan Sherburn, the millionaire, struggled for his life.

When he recovered his senses, he gazed about him in a stupefied manner, having lost all count of time, and unaware of what he had gone through.

He began to mutter, and raved at the absent Daly for neglecting him. He tried to move, but was unable to do so, and then he knew he was very ill. The first sight of the nurse bending over him with her kind, sympathetic face, gave him a start. It was a long time since he remembered any woman looking at him like that.   It reminded him of his mother, whose spoilt darling he had been.

'Who are you ?   What are you doing here ?' he asked in a low voice.

'I am your nurse,' she said softly.   'You have been dangerously ill, and are so still. You must keep quiet.'

He was silent for some minutes, and then he asked : 'Has anyone been to see me ?'

'No,' replied the nurse ; 'but your friends do not know you are so ill.'

'Does my wife know ?' he asked.

'Yes,' said the nurse ; 'she requested me to write and let her know how you were going on.'

'Very kind of her,' sneered Sherburn. 'She's waiting for me to peg out, I suppose ; but I'm not going to, just to spite her.   You may write and tell her so.'

The nurse felt shocked.   She knew nothing of Morgan Sherburn and his wasted life.   Had she done so, it would have made no difference to her : she would have fought for him with death, as duty bade her.

'Of course, you don't know,' said Sherburn. 'It's just as well you are ignorant of the facts. You are a good woman, are you not ?'

'I try to do my duty, sir,' she said.

'Let me look at your face,' he said.

She bent over him and looked at him kindly,

fearlessly, the look of a woman who knew naught of the Lady Bettys of this world.

Sherburn sighed. Something in the nurse's face made him think.

'You're not afraid of me ?' he asked curiously.

'Oh dear no !' she said, smiling.

'That's because you do not know my character,' he said.

'It would make no difference,' she said. 'I am nursing you, not your character.'

'Well I'm—surprised,' he said, changing the word he was about to use. It was the first time in his life since his mother died that a woman's look had checked his unruly tongue.

'Let me make you comfortable,' she said, and commenced to rearrange the pillows.

The idea of anyone troubling to make him comfortable seemed to amuse Sherburn. Although a millionaire, he had none of the love which brings the comfort many a poor man possesses.

'Am I very ill ?' he asked.

'Yes,' said the nurse.

A long paused ensued. Morgan Sherburn felt frightened. At last he braced up his nerves to ask the question :

'Shall I get better ?' and looked at the nurse eagerly.

'I hope so,' she replied cheerfully ; 'but you

must be very careful, and do exactly as you are told.'

'I don't think there's much chance for me,' he said in a trembling voice; 'I feel—I feel jolly bad. Where's Daly?'

'Shall I ring for him?' asked the nurse.

'Yes.'

Raymond Daly came into the room. He had not seen Morgan Sherburn since he recovered his senses. The nurse said to him:

'Mr. Sherburn is quite conscious now, and wishes to see you.'

Raymond Daly went to the bedside and looked at Sherburn. There was no pity or sympathy in the valet's face.

'Tell the nurse to go away,' said Sherburn.

'You are to leave the room,' said Daly to the nurse.

'I will go in here,' she said, opening the door of the dressing-room. 'Call me at once if you see any sign of weakness in him. He ought not to be allowed to talk.'

'Daly, I'm going to cave in,' said Sherburn. 'I've ridden my last race. I've not been a bad master to you. I've let you fleece me fairly well, and no doubt you have feathered your nest.'

Raymond Daly shook his head, and said:

'You've been a hard master, but not a bad master to *me*.'

20

'Which means I have been to others,' said Sherburn. 'There's something I want you to do.'

'What is it?' said Daly.

'Tell Sir Gordon Sefton all about that telegram.'

'I'm hanged if I do!' said Daly. 'A nice hole he'd put me into.'

'Sir Gordon would not harm you,' said Sherburn. 'He would merely regard you as my tool in the matter.'

'I daren't do it,' said Daly.

'You must,' said Sherburn. 'I'll haunt you to your dying day if you do not. I'll make it worth your while—I'll give you a thousand pounds if you will go to Sefton and tell Sir Gordon.'

'A thousand pounds?' said Daly.

'Yes,' said Sherburn; 'and you must go to-day.'

'How about the money?' asked Daly.

'You shall have it when you return with Sir Gordon,' said Sherburn; 'you must ask him to come back with you, and bring my wife. Tell him I wish to see my wife before I die.'

'You'll not die,' said Daly; 'but I'll do what you wish. I'll go—— Nurse! nurse!' he called.

Morgan Sherburn had fainted. The nurse ran to his bedside and at once took means to restore him to consciousness. In a few minutes Sherburn came round.

'You must not talk,' said the nurse. 'I shall not leave you again.'

'Go at once,' said Sherburn to the valet; and Daly left the room.

Morgan Sherburn was restless during the remainder of the day and night. His past life came vividly before him, and he shuddered at the thought of all he had done and of what he had left undone. When he was well and strong, and going the pace headlong, he thought but little of religion. He had been blessed, or cursed, with an enormous fortune, which he had used in the devil's work. He racked his brain to think of one good action free from any taint of selfishness he had done, and found none. All his money had been lavished on the gratification of his own passions, and he had caused others to sin with him. Now he knew that millions would not buy him what he wanted—a contented mind, a fearless heart to meet what lay before him. His millions could not buy him love, respect, honour, and peace. They might buy him the luxuries of this life until he needed such things no more. A sudden thought occurred to him as he wondered what would become of the money he left behind : would it be squandered as he had squandered it ? He might prevent that, at any rate. If he had done no good with his millions when alive, might not others do good with them when he was gone ? Then his somewhat wandering thoughts rambled in a different direction. There was Lady Betty and Portsdown. A savage exultation came over him as he thought that if he died Portsdown would lose his ten thousand. This was a consolation, at any rate. Lady Betty had drained his purse deeply, and must be satisfied. No more of his wealth should filter into that channel. He laughed a hoarse laugh that startled the watchful nurse as he pictured to himself the expression upon Portsdown's face when he heard of his death. To lose ten thousand pounds when it was well-nigh in his grasp would be almost too much for Portsdown. Then Morgan Sherburn dozed for a couple of hours, and his dulled brain was tenanted by prize-fights, races, brawls, and bogus telegrams, all jumbled together in a startling manner. He awoke suddenly, and felt a clammy sweat upon his face. He cried out in his fear, and the nurse, placing a steady hand upon his brow, soothed him to rest again.

The next day Sir Gordon Sefton and Ena arrived at the house. Raymond Daly had told the shameful story of the telegram, and Sir

Gordon had with difficulty refrained from kicking him out of the house. Ena was persuaded to accompany her father to London.

'You must go,' said her mother. 'I do not believe Morgan Sherburn will die, but he is dangerously ill, and is repenting of his misdeeds. Your father has made Raymond Daly write a full account of how this slander was brought about and circulated, and you have nothing more to fear on that account. Go with your father, Ena. It is your duty, for this man is your husband, and you ought to see him.'

So Ena accompanied her father, and again entered the house in Park Lane where she had suffered many indignities.

During the journey to London Ena had been silent. She thought perhaps she had been wrong in her handling of Morgan Sherburn. She married him, knowing his character, and, instead of trying to reform him, she had taken her own course, and let him go his way. She had held aloof from her husband during that unhappy honeymoon, and had behaved as though they were unmarried—nay, more, as though they were hardly friends. She knew she had the power to fascinate Morgan Sherburn, and chain him to her side. She shuddered at the thought of it then, even as she did now, but nevertheless, having married him, she felt

some of that power ought to have been exercised over him.   Might she not have reclaimed
him to some extent ?   Was it entirely his fault
that he left her during the honeymoon ?   Would
not a few words from her have kept him with
her ?   These questions Ena was honest enough
to answer against herself.   Her own heart told
her she had regarded Morgan Sherburn as
totally bad, and had not even searched for
an atom of better nature in him.   Such thoughts
as these made her feel more lenient towards
him than she otherwise would have done when
she entered her husband's house.

Morgan Sherburn was anxiously awaiting
their arrival, and desired them to be sent to
him as early as possible.

' I will see him first,' said Ena, much to her
father's surprise.

Sir Gordon rather fancied he would have
been requested to pave the way for Ena, and
was much relieved in consequence.

She followed the maid upstairs, and the nurse
opened the door for her.

' Hush ! he is asleep,' said the nurse.   Ena
entered the room quietly.   The nurse thought :
' What a beautiful woman, and how proud !'

Ena went to her husband's bedside, and
looked at him.   A feeling of pity and sorrow
for him and his wasted life took possession of

her, and she showed an emotion she could not control. She stood gazing at him for some time, and then he awoke and saw her.

'It is very good of you to come to me,' he said. 'Can you forgive me?'

For answer she bent over him and kissed him. It was the first kiss she had ever given him. He had snatched kisses from her, and felt her shudder as he took them.

'Why did you not kiss me like that before, Ena?' he said. 'Things might have been different then.'

She bowed her head and did not speak, for she knew he spoke the truth.

CHAPTER XXX.

THE RICH WIDOW.

ENA SHERBURN remained alone with her husband for some time. He told her many things that surprised her they were so totally foreign to his nature as she had understood it. She felt she ought to do as he requested, although she had much objection to taking what he offered.

Morgan Sherburn decided to leave the whole of his vast wealth to his wife, with the exception of a few legacies to certain people who had not been so rapacious as many of the toadies who had surrounded him.   Ena raised strenuous objections to this course, but Sherburn was firm.

'You know I am dying,' he said ; 'do not refuse my request.   It will ease my mind to know you will make good use of my money. It has done me more harm than good, and I want you to repair some of the damage I have done.   I feel in a forgiving frame of mind.   I can even forgive Dudley Massie.'   Ena could not help blushing slightly at the mention of his name ; and Sherburn said, with a faint smile 'I have done him no great wrong, Ena.   I was jealous of him, for I felt it was only your pride made you accept me in preference to Massie.   I acknowledge I hated him, because I thought you loved him.   Do you love him ?' he asked eagerly.

'No,' said Ena firmly ; 'I do not love Mr. Massie.   He is a stanch friend, but nothing more.   He never will be anything more to me.'

Morgan Sherburn gave a sigh of satisfaction. It was a bitter thought to him that when he was gone Ena might marry Massie, who would thus enjoy his (Sherburn's) wealth.   He believed his wife when she said she did not love Massie, and it soothed him.

'Of course you will marry again ?' he said.

'I do not think so,' she replied.

'You will be sought after for your wealth.

You can command any rank with the wealth I shall leave you. You would make a splendid duchess, Ena.' Her eyes glistened. She loved power. 'You are very proud,' he went on, 'and very cold. There will be no danger in my leaving you all my money, for I know you will not throw it away upon some worthless man. You have had experience of a worthless man, have you not?'

'We will not talk of such things,' she said. 'I will do all I can to carry out your wishes. I am very sorry I have not helped you more. Had I given you encouragement, you might have been different.'

'You are right,' he said. 'It is the want of love at home that makes such men as I seek a spurious substitute for it elsewhere.'

Raymond Daly entered the room, and, with a curious look at Ena, said :

'May I have a word with Mr. Sherburn?'

'Speak out,' said Sherburn. 'There is nothing my wife may not hear.' Still Daly hesitated, and Ena was about to retire, when Sherburn said : 'Do not leave me. We have been separated too long. Now, Daly, what is it?'

'Her ladyship has called,' said Daly.

Ena drew herself up proudly, and looked haughtily at Daly.

'Tell her ladyship Mr. Sherburn's wife is

here ; also tell her that Mr. Sherburn is dangerously ill, and that she is requested not to call again.'

Daly looked at Morgan Sherburn, who said

'Give the message to her exactly as you have been told.'

' I will,' said Daly ; and he did. And Lady Betty felt hot and cold all over ; but she went away, thinking she would see Morgan Sherburn again when he recovered, and that then she would have her revenge.

' I am sorry,' said Sherburn.

Ena shrugged her shoulders. Her heart hardened against her husband at the mere thought of Lady Betty.

' Send Sir Gordon to me,' said Sherburn ; and Ena left him, and went to her father.

Sir Gordon Sefton had been much shocked at Sherburn's appearance when he first saw him, and he thought now he was gradually getting worse.

' I want you to see my lawyer at once, and bring him here,' said Sherburn. ' I want to add a codicil to my will ; please go at once. I had rather you went, because more notice will be taken of my request.'

Sir Gordon drove to Sir Henry Lewin's offices, and found the old lawyer in. When he stated why he had come, Sir Henry said :

'Are you sure he is dying?'

'I think there can be no doubt about it.'

'Then I will accompany you myself,' said Sir Henry. 'His present will is scandalous and iniquitous. I have many times endeavoured to induce him to alter it. I hope the codicil he intends to add will entirely reverse the will as it now stands. At present, it is an insult to his wife, and a disgrace to himself.'

They were quickly at Park Lane, and Sir Henry Lewin saw Morgan Sherburn at once. He was shocked at his client's appearance.

'You are surprised to see me like this,' said Sherburn; 'I'm going under, Sir Henry. I've been a bad lot, but I'm trying to make some amends.'

When Sir Henry Lewin heard Morgan Sherburn's intention of leaving nearly the whole of his wealth to his wife, he was surprised and pleased.

'Then, you wish to cancel the former will?'

'Yes,' said Sherburn.

'It will not take long to draft such a codicil as you require,' said Sir Henry. 'Very few vast fortunes have been disposed of in such a simple manner.'

'Give Raymond Daly a thousand pounds,' said Sherburn; 'I owe it him.'

Sir Henry looked doubtful.

'You mean he has squeezed it out of you?'

'Not in this case,' said Sherburn, with the ghost of a smile. 'I also want you to pay Michael Malone five hundred pounds.'

A look of disgust passed over the lawyer's face.

'Of course I'll do it; but I really don't care about it.'

'You know who I mean?' asked Sherburn.

'Yes; the man who beat Dusky Jim.'

'You saw the fight?'

'I did,' said Sir Henry; 'and lost my money.'

'That is the reason you do not care about Malone having the money. He's a decent chap, is Mick, quite a different man from the black-guards I've been amongst,' said Sherburn.

'Anything else for me to pay out?' asked Sir Henry.

'No,' said Sherburn.

The codicil to Morgan Sherburn's will was duly executed, signed, and witnessed, and these few lines made Ena Sherburn at her husband's death one of the richest women in England.

Pressure having been put upon him by Sir Gordon, Dudley Massie came to see Sherburn, accompanied by Fred Lostock. A gleam of hatred came into Sherburn's eyes as he saw the man who had beaten him in that never-to-be-forgotten Grand National, and some of the old feelings against his wife and Massie, that prompted him to act as he did, were roused in him. After a time, however, he calmed down, shook hands with Massie, and said good-bye.

'Will you accept Snowstorm from me?' said Sherburn.

'If it will please you,' replied Massie.

'It will very much,' said Sherburn; and so Dudley Massie became possessed of Snowstorm.

Morgan Sherburn died quietly in his bed, and not, as many of his so-called friends had prophesied he would, 'in a ditch.' His will came as a shock to many people. That he should have left his vast wealth to his wife absolutely was a nine days' wonder.

'There's no telling what a fellow will do when he's passing in his cheques,' said Fred Lostock.

To Dudley Massie the news of Ena's inheritance came as a shock. He recognised at once that whatever hopes he had entertained of one day winning Ena were dashed for ever. Her wealth put a barrier between them, for he knew Ena's nature too well to flatter himself she would look upon him with any favour now.

'Nothing less than a duke will satisfy her,' he thought bitterly.

Ena Sherburn was possessed by a feeling of exultation as she heard the will read that made her mistress of so much money. She felt she really could forgive Morgan Sherburn now he

had made such ample amends.   Sherburn being
dead no doubt made a difference in her feelings
towards him.   It is wonderful how forgiving
such a woman as Ena can be, when the object
of her forgiveness has ' ceased from troubling.'

When Arthur Sefton heard of his sister's
good fortune, he said :

' She doesn't deserve it; she married Morgan
Sherburn for his money, and she's got what
she bargained for.   It is an encouragement to
other women to go and do likewise, and I
don't approve of it.'

This was his opinion as propounded to
Dudley Massie.

' There's one gleam of hope in it, however,'
went on Arthur : ' it puts her out of your reach.
When you see what " side " Ena puts on, you'll
wonder how ever you were such a fool as to
think about her.   Then you'll blot her out of
your mind, and your eyes will wander in search
of some other fair damsel, and will naturally
alight upon Beatrice.   Having once fixed your
gaze in that direction, my friend, keep it there,
and don't go wandering in search of other
attractions.   On the whole, when I come to
think of it, I'm rather glad Ena has come into
such beastly wealth.   I shall be able to negotiate a loan with her, on the strength of my
future prospects, when I have backed a loser.

Do you know, Dudley, I believe Sherburn gave you Snowstorm in the hope that one day you might break your neck on him !'

Dudley Massie laughed as he replied :

' Snowstorm is not the sort of horse I shall break my neck by coming to grief on him. He fences too well for that. I believe he's better than The Slogger.'

' Say that again and I'll cut your acquaintance !' said Arthur. ' The Slogger is a hero.'

When Lord Portsdown heard of Morgan Sherburn's death, he came nearer to having an apoplectic fit than ever he was in his life. He had withdrawn proceedings against Lady Betty, and had indignantly denied in print that there was any truth in the rumour that he was about to bring an action for divorce against his wife. And after paying stiffish sums for such announcements out of his own pocket, he was minus his reward of ten thousand. ' Porty ' had never had such a bad or richly deserved fall before.

Lady Betty was full of wrath against the dead man and the living widow, especially the latter. The idea of Ena Sherburn rolling in wealth was most obnoxious to Lady Betty. The mere fact of Morgan Sherburn leaving all his money to his wife was a sufficient refutation of the slanders that had been circulated about her. Lady Betty was jeered at by her acquaintances, who cut out all the smart paragraphs about 'the beautiful and enormously wealthy widow,' and posted them to her in delicately-perfumed envelopes. 'Porty' harangued her in a lofty manner, and nearly drove her frantic by dwelling upon the generosity he had displayed towards her.

Ena Sherburn had thousands upon thousands of pounds, and Lady Betty could not make both ends meet, and did not attempt to do so. This was quite enough to drive a more saint-like woman than Lady Betty to the verge of distraction.

What use Ena Sherburn made of her vast wealth time will tell. Her sister, Beatrice Sefton, is of a different mould, and does not envy Ena her wealth. She still has hopes in a certain direction, which Arthur Sefton does his utmost to encourage. She has learned to wait as well as hope, and probably, when he has quite got over his infatuation, Dudley Massie will turn in her direction. Beatrice knows, if the time ever comes when Dudley Massie asks her to be his wife, that he will love her above all other women. For that time she is contented to wait.

THE END.

www.ingramcontent.com/pod-product-compliance
Lightning Source LLC
Chambersburg PA
CBHW020952030726
47496CB00005B/1482